Nine From The Ninth

Nine From The Ninth

Paul A. Newman
Bob Wallace
Jack Bick

*To Richard and Nancy —
With affection and personal gratitude for our more than three decades of friendship.
Bob Wallace
February 2003*

Writers Club Press
New York Lincoln Shanghai

Nine From The Ninth

All Rights Reserved © 2002 by Paul A. Newman

No part of this book may be reproduced or transmitted in any form or by any means, graphic, electronic, or mechanical, including photocopying, recording, taping, or by any information storage retrieval system, without the written permission of the publisher.

Writers Club Press
an imprint of iUniverse, Inc.

For information address:
iUniverse, Inc.
2021 Pine Lake Road, Suite 100
Lincoln, NE 68512
www.iuniverse.com

ISBN: 0-595-25305-9 (pbk)
ISBN: 0-595-65084-8 (cloth)

Printed in the United States of America

This book is dedicated to the Rangers from Co E, 75th Infantry Rangers, 9th Infantry Division, who died in combat in 1969.

Richard Bellwood
January 18, 1949–January 25, 1969

Roman Gale Mason
September 25, 1947–January 27, 1969

Leon David Moore
August 24, 1947–January 27, 1969

Richard V. Thompson
June 12, 1947–January 27, 1969

Irwin Leon Edelman
December 17, 1944–February 18, 1969

Warren Lizotte, Jr.
August 20, 1948–February 26, 1969

Lonnie Dale Evans
December 26, 1949–April 10, 1969

Michael Volheim
November 8, 1948–May 29, 1969

Curtis Ray Daniels
November 2, 1946–May 29, 1969

Herbert Frost
June 26, 1937–June 21, 1969

Contents

Preface ix

The Yankee 1
    by Paul A. Newman

Staff Sergeant Frost 15
    by Bob Wallace

Kill Them All 35
    by Jack Bick

Kodak Moments 43
    by Bob Wallace

Smart Charlie 59
    By Jack Bick

A More Than Typical Non-Mission Day 67
aka: The Shitter
    by Paul A. Newman

Nine Lessons From The Ninth 81
    by Bob Wallace

The Rules of War 99
    by Jack Bick

The Bo Bo Canal 105
    by Paul A. Newman

Epilogue 129
About the Authors 131

Preface

War stories have been in existence ever since the Bible began. Wars of the United States have been few in the realm of history. As our Second World War Veterans are passing, the Korean War is taking the front in publicity—The Forgotten War. But in the minds of most of the populace, The Vietnam War was the last traditional war fought by the United States. For Rangers of the Co. E, 75th Inf, 9th Inf. Division, Vietnam was their only war.

These nine stories by these three authors comprise a point of view. The Vietnam war was immediate to them. It was a daily task. And, it was daily pleasure. They were young men, then. And, being young, they had more energy than they knew what to do with. That energy was channeled by the politicians, Defense Department, and Brass into a lean, mean, fighting machine.

The Rangers were proud of the designation of "Ranger". It meant something personal, some accomplishment. The best of the best. Elite. Merrill's Marauders. LRRP had the same aura. Other soldiers looked at these Rangers as crazy and with envy. Why would any sane person go looking for trouble? To a certain extent, they were crazy. To go into enemy territory with only six men, announce your entrance by helicopter, and sit and wait for the enemy. Yes, that is a little crazy. But, part of the crazy was the antics when they were not in the field. Personality crazy. There were some real nuts, fun nuts, in that unit. The times at the base camp were, in retrospect, quite joyous, quite entertaining;

movies, steak roasts, camaraderie, and a pool room with beer for only twenty-five cents. Of course the beer was Falstaff a lot of the time, but we got used to that quite easily.

More important, were the relationships between the troopers. Lifetime bonds created under absolute stress and terror. Persons who failed to perform in the field were *persona non grata,* and treated as such until they left. Friendships formed ultra tensile strength bonds. These were guys to die for; and, some did.

These nine stories are true; and, they are not true. Admittedly, where necessary, names have been changed. No one wants to get into trouble, no one wants to unnecessarily hurt anyone's feelings thirty-two years after the fact, and no one wants others to think ill of anyone else with whom they served. And so, names were changed. Some of you will recognize yourselves and say, "Oh boy, that was me. I can't believe he thought of me that way." Others may not recognize themselves. After all, time, distance, and our own ages dim our memories. What is of great attraction and personal interest to one, may be nothing to another. In speaking to Bob Wallace (Governor) about certain missions on which we were together, our impressions are completely different. Obviously, it was perspective. And, of course, to me, my perspective was the correct one.

So, as you read these stories, remember, it is the author's perspective. From the author's view, with thirty-two years added on, actions are sometimes shed, names are forgotten, and certain details may be included that occurred on a different mission or at different time. After all, these are stories, not specific historic documents. In order to make a story cohesive, details must be added. There are literary attributes to which attention must be given. The story must be complete; you don't want to leave the reader hanging. In this manner, some of the stories utilize a modicum of literary license. Please keep that in mind.

The Rangers were lean, muscled men. Fights occurred. When the Transportation Company across the road came over and made drunken demands, the entire group at the open air movies jumped into the fray. There were twenty fights going on at once. And, we kicked their butts. I recall the raucous reminiscing while I cooked beans over a heat tab watching the rest of the movie after the fight. "Wow, that was great" was the feeling. And, the infamous Crawford-Tex fight. It was a build-up of months; and, they lived up to their reputations. What a great time, in retrospect. But, you are not reading this preface to hear my war stories; they are written herein.

The three authors have kept in touch these last thirty-two years. They went on R & R together to Hong Kong in 1969. Bob Wallace and Jack Bick went on R & R to Japan for their second R & R and visited Paul Newman at Camp Drake Hospital where he was convalescing from his war induced wounds. That friendship trilogy has persisted to this day. We attempt to get together every five years. We met at "The Wall" in DC. We bring our slides, photos and other accouterments together and reminisce. Our wives stay away. We dine at a Vietnamese restaurant. We eat more Vietnamese food now than we did in 1969. It is safer now, no glass, no gook trying to kill us. Vietnam was a large part of our lives. As our lives progress and the time of our living decreases, the importance of that year is inversely proportional. It is huge. We did something significant and it is our life. By golly, we fought for our country even if our country wimped out.

Vietnam today is a communist country—shit rolls downhill. Having revisited Vietnam in 1999, it was clear that the people in South Vietnam disliked and distrusted their communist government. Whereas, while we may distrust our government (an IRS audit perchance?), we love our country. We talked to many of the Veterans who spent one to fifteen years in re-education camps, who were not permitted to work and earn money after release from the camps, and who, given a gun, would willingly fight that government again. We re-visited Tan An. Saw the bridge over which we dragged the shitter which you will read about herein. We were unable to access Dong Tam because it is a military facility—what a surprise. The closest we got to Dong Tam was the Dong Tam Snake Farm located next door—Bob

Wallace actually allowed a python of twelve feet in length to be wrapped around him. I have the photograph to prove it.

We walked into the remote areas where we used to sneak and peek. Our presence, this time, was welcome. We were invited in for tea; hot tea on a ninety-five degree day still makes me sweat profusely. The people were gracious, interested, and gathered around us to ask a million questions. We had an interpreter with us, not a *chu hoi*. The feeling of *deja vu* walking along a dike with the nipa-palm brushing against my arms sent chills up my spine. But, what an exhilarating feeling. In the vernacular of the day—it was a "rush." The entire visit was a rush. I must admit, there was a certain apprehension dwelling in me as we approached the country. But, after a day, when I discovered that I was one of many tourists, that apprehension dissolved. We did not see many Americans visiting Vietnam; and, that was ok with us. The country was still pristine, in a touristy sort of way.

We rented a sampan, an operator, and an interpreter to traverse the canals from Ben Tre and My Tho. The Mekong River looks bigger than I remember it. A mighty river. We saw not one footbridge wrecked by troops. In fact, the logs across the canals were in tip top shape. We saw no bunkers. We refused to go to Chu Chi to see the tunnels, but we did go to the War Museum in Saigon to evidence the continued hatred of the communist government against the USA. They took Visa and Master Card at the museum gift shop, though—the true winner in the war.

I invite you to read these stories and to experience our experiences. To enjoy, to anger, to remember the little detail you forgot, to get rid of your continued "case of the ass", and to rejoice in the belief that you, a Ranger of the Co. E, 75th Inf., 9th Inf. Division did what you did.

Paul A. Newman

Acknowledgments

The authors thank Hilan Jones for all the effort he has dedicated to Co E, 75th Infantry, Rangers and the publication of the periodic newsletter.

We thank our wives who have facilitated the friendships between the fellows.

We thank all of the members of our teams who protected for our backs.

The Yankee

by Paul A. Newman

Sergeant Newman had CQ (charge of quarters) duty that Friday. It started at 1600 hours and continued until 0800 the next morning. He had never been CQ before, he participated in too many missions. When a ranger came off a mission, he had the following day free of duty, so he could sleep. However, his team 2-1 had not been on a mission for three days and he was selected for CQ.

The duties of the CQ were self explanatory. He was in charge of quarters. He made command decisions unless he thought they were so outside his range of competence that he had to ask for guidance. In that case he would wake the First Sergeant or the Company Commander. His first choice would be the First Sergeant, more approachable and more accessible.

Newman had been in country for little more than four months. Promoted to E-5 rapidly, he was given a team, which consisted of five men and himself. He was promoted too quickly, according to several of the men from the other teams. His team was assistant team leader and four young men.

Six teams comprised the base camp contingent at Dong Tam, Vietnam, along with three teams at Bear Cat and three teams at Tan An.

The main operations emanated from Dong Tam. And, unfortunately for the men, with so many teams, and such limited resources for missions, idle teams were assigned work details such as building bunkers; making sure the flow of water during the wet season flowed away from the barracks area; maintaining the bridges over the moat surrounding the company area; and burning shit. But, luckily, for Newman, Sergeants only had to supervise the details, not participate. Although, he did participate—most of the time, except for burning shit.

The CQ stayed in the command bunker the entire night. It housed the offices of the Company Commander, the First Sergeant, and the company's communications. A fifty foot antenna extended above the bunker which was eighteen feet by forty feet, with perimeter walls lined with six by six posts enclosing dirt and sand three feet in width. It was hoped that the walls would protect the command post in the event of a mortar or rocket attack. The roof was three feet thick of the same material. A solid, hoped for, impregnable structure. This building had already been built when Newman came into the company. But he helped supervise the building of an identical building, not quite finished, to mirror the command bunker. Electricity powered the fans and air conditioning to keep the bunker cool and ventilated.

Newman was looking forward to a quiet, cool evening. Only one team was going out on a mission. The radio operator, who was under Newman's command for the evening, would handle most of the radio transmissions. The artillery coordination was pre-plotted with the coordinates pasted on a pad with grease pencil. The Cavalry squadron was on call for any immediate extractions, if the team was compromised, ambushed, or otherwise in trouble.

Newman was to report at 1530 hours to get his instructions and the information on the inserting team. He checked his uniform, camouflage pants and jacket with sergeant stripes pinned to his collars. The camouflage shoulder patch on the left shoulder read "Co. E, 75th Inf. (Ranger)". Polished, but not shined, boots; pants tucked up with an elastic band over the boots; he then put on his black beret with the

Ranger flash. The flash was a derivation of the insignia utilized by Merrill's Marauders known for their deep penetration in Burma in the Second World War. It looked sharp. He looked in the mirror, he looked a cool, lean, mean, fighting ranger. He liked looking lean and mean and efficient.

Newman closed the screen door to his room. Sergeants, who were team leaders, got their own room, small, but private. He walked the two hundred feet across the company parade ground to the command bunker. Three rangers sat drinking at a picnic table at the corner of the command bunker. Newman noticed immediately that two were drunk. They laughed too loud, their movements too histrionic. One of the rangers, Sgt. Brooks, was derosing tomorrow. His tour of duty was up. He was short. His body was tall at six foot three, but his time was short. He was so short he could play handball on the curb.

Sgt. Brooks was what Newman thought of as a hillbilly. He was tall, thin, short brown hair, talked with a southern twang; didn't like Yankees and made it known that he didn't like Yankees. Newman was obviously a Yankee—from Cleveland at that. Neither Newman nor Brooks had ever spoken to each other in the four months that Newman had been in the company. They knew each other, but from Newman's perspective, the initial glance he got from Brooks told him they would never be friends. Newman had heard comments. "That damn Yankee. Those fucking Yankees. Yankee this…Yankee that." Brooks was obsessed with his hatred of Yankees. Forget the gooks, they weren't the real enemy, it was the Yankees. That damn Sherman destroyed the South. The South shall rise again.

Brooks had a confederate flag hanging over his bed in the barracks. With only one black member in the company, the flag did not become an issue. Brooks did speak to "the negro", as he called him. He liked Sgt. Brown, he was an okay negro. Knew his place, he did. Sgt. Brown stayed away from Brooks, especially when he was drinking, which was most of the time on his free time. They were not on the same team.

Newman acutely sensed he was going to have trouble with Brooks this night. Newman, a short but powerful five foot six, ignored Brooks's comment as he entered the command bunker: "Yankee, I'll be damned glad to get away from these fucking Yankees", and he raised his beer can in salute, smiling maliciously.

Brooks had on a white sleeveless undershirt, green camouflage pants, no hat. He was happy to DEROS. Get the hell out of this war. Get away from killing gooks. Get the hell away from all these damn Yankees. And that Newman, a fucking sergeant already, and a fucking team leader already. What the hell did he know. Was he there when Brooks and Small were the only two men alive after that ambush at the BoBo canal? Fuck no. A goddamn sergeant and a team leader. Little shit. Ought to kick his ass before I leave.

Brooks knew, but did not say, and in his drunken vivacity was unable to cogently comprehend, that he wasn't made team leader because of his stupid decisions in the field. He had shied and hid when the team was ambushed. As assistant team leader he failed to call for support in a timely manner after the team leader was hit. He lost it. He knew, but he did not say. It still pissed him off that this little shit Yankee made sergeant in less than four months. And a team leader at that. The others at the table also knew why, but did not say. Brooks was leaving tomorrow, let him go. He was entitled to a last drunk after a whole year of gooks. Tomorrow he will be free, jetting on home to pleasure and no Yankees—the real world.

Newman reported to the First Sergeant Press, a man in his fifties, several inches taller than Newman but less stocky, with pressed and starched fatigues tailored to fit. Three stripes up, three stripes down. He'd been in the Army a long time. A calm man, angered infrequently, took things in stride. He explained to Newman the commo room—a room with which Newman was very familiar, having been on numerous missions, and the details of the mission which would insert at 1800 hours. The men were getting ready for the mission,. Their inspection would occur in half an hour. The inspection was haphazard—if the men didn't know what they needed on a six man mission by this time, then God help them! They did know and inspections were cursory, at best, when they did occur. If anything, the men always took more ammunition or explosive devices than was necessary. In this way, they could blow the shit out of hooches or bunkers or anything they wanted before they extracted. And, if they didn't make contact or have to escape quickly, it was a fun thing to do. It honed your explosive skills and capitalized on Uncle Sam's generosity in providing this trip.

Newman was given the Cavalry Company's frequencies, the team's frequencies, Artillery's frequencies, the Mohawk's frequencies, and the jets, if necessary. Eight times out of ten, either Artillery or Cavalry gunships came to the rescue. Everyone enjoyed calling in the jets; they tried to get them to drop the bombs as close to their position as possible without being blown up themselves. He was given the priority list of contacts, then informed where the First Sergeant would be, the CO would be, and the FAC. The FAC, forward air controller, was the liaison between the team and CQ. The team was so far from Dong Tam that the radios didn't reach transmission. Therefore, the intermediary FAC handled the relay. Most of Newman's communication would be with the FAC. FAC would get the sit reps (situation reports) from the team leader or assistant. FAC would check with the team hourly and check in with Newman hourly. Not Newman directly, but his radio operator for the night, Specialist Fourth Class Sommers.

Newman had been in the Command Bunker for fifteen minutes and was preparing to leave. He stepped by the swinging gate which separated the First Sergeant's office from the waiting area, when he heard a commotion at the entrance to the building. Brooks and his two cronies were entering. Brooks had a beer in his hand, talking loudly. Newman sensed Brooks, observed the malicious flash in his eye, his extravagant movements. Brooks was very drunk. Brooks didn't like Newman. The First Sergeant saw Brooks and began to speak when Brooks "accidentally on purpose" bumped into Newman. What better way to get a blow in than to have it appear an accident.

The bump was forceful; Brooks dipped his shoulder to get better leverage, intending to try to knock Newman on his ass. Newman saw the bump coming. He absorbed it, stepped back with it and punched Brooks with his right fist in Brooks' right jaw. Brooks leaned over the railing, shocked. That little son of a bitch punched me. Shock, bewilderment, surprise. The audacity of the Yankee. Short, little Yankee. His mind fogged with alcohol, dimly and slowly, the shock turned to immediate insane anger. But even in his drunken anger, he knew not to jump Newman in the First Sergeant's office. And, anyways, this is what he was looking for—to fight Newman. A going away present for himself—a bonus. This will be better than the Seiko watch they gave me for surviving the year. Beat the shit out of this little sergeant Yankee. But the little shit had stuck first. Not expected. Now, it was not just a beating he was going to get, but some vindication also. Punch me first, asshole Yankee!

The First Sergeant saw Brooks bump into Newman. He wasn't sure if it was intentional or not; too close to call. Brooks was drunk. It was his last day. Give him some leeway. Just tell him to take it outside. But then Newman punched him. Not a second delay. He obviously thought it was intentional. He's CQ tonight, he doesn't have time for this shit.

"Outside with this!" bellowed the First Sergeant. "Not in here."

Newman looked at him. First Sergeant raised his hands, palms up, and said nothing. Let them sort it out by themselves. Maybe a test of leadership here. But not in my office.

"Com'on, mother fucker," screamed Brooks. "Right now, outside. This'll be the third battle of Bull Run, you fucking Yankee." He paused a moment, his anger seething and growing like a whirling tornado. Newman looked at him.

"Alright asshole!" Newman said quietly. "You want to fight, you got it."

The two Rangers with Brooks stared in astonishment at the entire process. They said not a word. After Newman agreed to fight, they turned and ran out the door yelling, "Fight, a fight!"

Newman waved Brooks to the door with a dismissal flip of the hand as if to say, lead on McDuff. But not a gentlemanly wave, more like a "get the hell outta here you filthy slime" wave. A short wave with arm slightly extended, palm downward, flicking out several times. The reverse of a di di mau sign to a gook.

Brooks interpreted the dismissal wave of Newman as just that. Out flotsam. Out jetsam. Out gook. And, it infuriated him. Alcohol and anger, anger and alcohol. The mix was good. Brooks was so angered he was nonsensical. His anger escalated, it pounded in his head. His florid face was beet red with fury.

Outside the Command Bunker was a railing separating the bunker from the parade ground. The railing had an opening at the doorway and Brooks stalked out into the bright sunlight thirty feet to the parade ground. The two cronies of Brooks had already garnered six spectators. Newman knew them. Everyone wanted to watch a fight no matter who was involved. Fights were fun to watch.

When Spec Four Wells fought Spec Four Campbell, the fight lasted thirty minutes. They were the best physically fit bodies in the company. They had been egged on to fight for months. Finally, Old Frosty, "The Legend of the Delta", as he liked to call himself before he was shot, got Wells so drunk and angry with lies told to him that Campbell supposedly had said, that the fight happened. The two were so evenly matched that they actually became friends afterwards. Newman knew that wouldn't happen here. No way would he ever be friends with Brooks. He hated the idea of Brooks: prejudiced, stupid, selfish, and good looking.

Brooks ripped off his tee shirt. Newman kept his on, but took off his camo shirt.

Newman appraised the situation. Big tall man, drunk. I can take advantage of his drunkenness, but his height and reach are much greater. Can't wait for him to have the advantage. Sober, he could probably kick the shit out of me. Drunk, we are more even. Couldn't let him get away with the insult, though. He did it on purpose. I don't care if it is his last day in country, I'm not going to take that shit. He's been looking for this Yankee for months.

Brooks approached Newman, his fists up. A huge grin crossed his face. His eyes danced with furious and malicious delight. Going to do damage to this short fucking Yankee. A little bad talk first.

"OK, you little fucking Yankee, how you want your medicine? Straight in or up your ass?"

Newman punched upwards. The only way he could connect with the jaw of Brooks was to punch upwards, and so he did. His punch, the right hand again, caused Brooks teeth to smack together. Trouble was, his tongue was between them. The stab of pain through the pain alleviating alcohol was a rush. His face screamed to his brain. It hurts. He took three steps backwards. This little Yankee shit has hit me again, first. What the fuck? Blood leaked down his chin. He spat. He saw some blood curl into a ball in the sand—his blood.

Brooks bellowed. A roar, unintelligible, anger, fury, a violent enthusiasm.

Newman had waited after his punch. It was a good punch, straight up, connected well. He must have bit his tongue. There goes french kissing his hillbilly girlfriend for the next week. Ha-ha. Next bout will be more serious.

Newman had wrestled in high school. He even had a scholarship to Bowling Green State University for wrestling, but his grades were so poor he dropped out after the first semester. However, he had won the intra-mural 140 lb tournament at BGSU before he dropped out. He was a fair wrestler. But Brooks needed something to stop him cold. Now that he has awakened and I have taken the first hit, he will get serious. Now I'm in trouble.

Brooks bellowed again and charged, swinging those long arms in arcing punches. Newman stepped into Brooks, did the wrestling move duck under to the left as Brooks' right arm extended to punch. Newman was behind Brooks, he wrapped his right arm across Brooks's stomach, his left arm grabbed Brooks's left arm at the triceps muscle, and he lifted Brooks, turning him to the left and tripping him so that he went down to the sand face first. Newman threw him down and immediately got up. He could wrestle him all day and win, but this was a fight, not a wrestling match.

Brooks got up, sand on his lips. Sand and blood mixed on his tongue, Brooks kept moving his tongue to get the sand off. Newman smiled at him. Brooks bellowed again, but more reserved this time. Pull the anger back a little. This is a fight. This little shit Yankee is pulling some tricks that weren't expected. Thought I was going to demolish him in the first flurry of punches. Get close to him and pound him. Don't let go. Pound him. Sand on my lips, shit!

Brooks wiped his lips with his arm. Stood up, appraised Newman. He's a little shit, how's he doing this to me?

Positioning himself into a boxing stance, Brooks punched at Newman, several glancing blows. Newman punched Brooks twice in the stomach, straight shots. One in the plexus, out of breath. Suck it in. Pull air in your lungs. Lucky punch. Grab the SOB

Brooks lunged and grabbed Newman in a hug, then punched him on the back, into his ribs. Newman lifted Brooks's legs and dumped him in the sand on his back. Brooks didn't let go. Newman slid from him. Brooks jumped up, ran at Newman, but halted a second before him and then grabbed him again. They had moved to the rail in front of the Command Bunker.

Newman saw there were twenty or so Rangers watching. Brooks collided with Newman, who turned Brooks so his back collided into the railing. Newman pushed Brooks, who was top heavy and apparently didn't know that the center of gravity of a body is the hips, over the railing, and then, because Brooks wouldn't let go, dragged him back across the railing scraping his back on the edge. Brooks fell. He got up and Newman punched him in the side of the face before he could fully stand. Brooks fell again.

Newman looked at the First Sergeant and said between his panting breaths, "How long do I have to do this, Sarge?"

First Sergeant understood. Brooks was too drunk to know he was beat. He kept coming and he kept getting beat down. Time to clear the mess.

"Acton, Glasser, get Brooks. That's enough! I mean it. Now! Brooks! You hear me? That's enough!" Yelled the First Sergeant.

Brooks hesitated, screamed unintelligibly, then started for Newman. Acton and Glasser jumped in and grabbed him.

"Take him to his bunk. That's enough. Make sure he quiets down."

The First Sergeant went to the Command Bunker. Newman went to his room. Acton and Glasser escorted Brooks towards the barracks. His back was scraped raw from being dragged across the railing. He was screaming, raising his head in the air, "you mother fucker, you mother fucking Yankee, I'm going to kill you." They dragged him away, fighting.

Newman straightened his clothing, changed his shirt, sweaty and dirty, with Brooks juice all over it. Fucking drunken hillbilly. He looked in the mirror, adjusted his shirt, combed his hair and exited towards the Command Bunker.

"Well," said the First Sergeant, "that was a nice break. Now we can get down to business. You OK?"

"Yeah, sure, Sarge."

"Alright, I hope he doesn't give you any trouble the rest of the night. We don't need that."

"I'll let you know if he does."

"Yeah, do that." The First Sergeant left.

*   *   *   *

Spec Four Wallace came into the Command Bunker. Looked at Newman. "Heard you had some activity?"

"Yeah, Brooks. Wants to kick my ass. Cocksucker's drunk. We had a little 'to do'."

"I heard. Sounds like you took care of him."

"Sure."

"I also heard he is still itching for you. He's screaming like a banshee in the barracks. I'd keep a lookout. The guy is crazy drunk."

"Yeah, I will."

*   *   *   *

The team had gone to the heliport for its mission. All radio communication was perfected. Newman was sipping coffee in the hopes it would help keep him awake all night. Suddenly, Brooks came crashing in to the Command Bunker. He hollered at Newman: "Com'on mother fucking Yankee. It's now. I say now." He stood at the rail. Newman looked at him. Here he is, CQ with duties to perform and this asshole calls him out to fight. He can't get into a fight while he is on CQ. He'll be busted for sure. How the hell does he handle this. Say no, I guess.

"Can't do it, Brooks. I'm on CQ. Tomorrow."

"Won't be no tomorrow, Yankee!" He spit straight at Newman, it fell short. "It's now, outside or I'm coming over the rail to kill you." He stared at Newman, drunk, malice, hatred, insanity.

Where were Acton and Glasser? What the hell happened to them? They were supposed to be watching Brooks. What to do now? Can't fight in the Bunker, too much electronic equipment. Too dangerous for the men out on the mission. Got a team out there. Can't reason with this asshole. How about if I go out and hit him a few times, maybe knock him out, so I can properly finish my duties. Can't get past him without a fight. Got to do it. Only way out.

"Ok, but not in here. Outside." He turned to the radio operator and hissed, "Get the First Sergeant, quickly."

Brooks led out. No one was outside. It was still light outside. 1930 hours, men at the bar, too light for the movies to be shown, where was everyone? Mess was over. Jesus, I'm going to have to fight this drunken asshole again.

Brooks wasn't going to let Newman get the first punch this time. As soon as Newman cleared the rail outside the Command Bunker, Brooks rushed, punching, catching Newman a solid fist to the side of the head. Newman went for the stomach, punched twice, thrice, six times before Brooks could get another punch. Brooks gagged. Leaned on the rail, vomited. Newman punched him in the side of the face, Brooks fell, threw up with his face in the sand. The First Sergeant grabbed Newman. "Back in the Bunker, Now!" Newman went into the bunker, sat down. He waited.

Five minutes later the First Sergeant came into the Command Bunker. "He won't bother you again. I specifically gave instructions that someone was to stay with him all night. All night. God damn Acton. I told him to watch him." First Sergeant snorted, angrily.

"You Ok?" He looked at Newman.

"Yeah, just pissed. Nothing I could do. No one was here. Pisses me off, Sarge." Newman wiped his brow.

* * * *

At 2100 hours the team FAC relayed the sit rep. Team ok, all quiet. No movement. Ambush set up on a trail. Lot of footprints. Call in an hour.

At 2130 hours, Newman heard a commotion outside, yelling, some conflict. He went to the door of the bunker. Brooks was in the center of the parade ground with an M-16. Newman knew there was a magazine in it. Acton and Glasser were coming up behind Brooks, stealthily. They were going to tackle him. Newman saw at a glance, Brooks wanted to kill him. He shut the door to the Command Bunker so he was not backlit and moved five paces to the right. Only low lights were on in the area, sufficient to move around and find your way without a flashlight. Brooks was yelling: "Come out you mother fucking Yankee! Come out, I'm going to blow your lights out, you fucking gook."

Brooks was nuts. Acton and Glasser were ten feet away. If Brooks saw them, he might shoot them. Newman yelled: "You asshole hillbilly!" And moved another ten feet to the right around the corner of the Bunker. Brooks took aim and Acton tackled him. The M-16 went flying. Brooks screamed, howled, scrambled. Acton and Glasser punched. They dragged Brooks away.

Newman went to his room, got his 45 caliber pistol with pistol belt, loaded it, put a round in the chamber even though it was against the company policy to have a chambered round in the company area and went back to the Command Bunker.

The First Sergeant came in ten minutes later, glanced at the pistol holster, ignored it, and said: "It won't happen again. You won't have to use it. We tied him to the bunk until 0800 hours. It's an order."

"Sarge, I will. No shit. I ain't putting up with it."

The First Sergeant looked at him gravely, nodded slightly and grinned.

"So tell me Sarge," Newman stroked his chin as if he was in deep thought, "help me with my history here. What war are we fighting?"

"Good question," said the First Sergeant, and left.

The team had no activity during the night. They were extracted at 0900 hours. Communication was perfect.

Sgt. Brooks got picked up by the jeep which took him to the helipad. He couldn't talk for the damage to his tongue. His face was sorely bruised on the lips and the side of the cheek. He snarled at Newman. He looked good to DEROS.

Staff Sergeant Frost

by Bob Wallace

This war story is not necessarily accurate in detail. It is a true story about a Long Range Reconnaissance Patrol (LRRP) team that operated in the Vietnam Delta between 1968-1970. If, as some believe, truth is an early casualty of war, those who experience combat understand how microscopic precision disembowels stories that capture war's essence. Just as great rivers with names like Mississippi, Amazon and Mekong cannot be understood by sediment analysis, military history will fail to capture the collective souls of the few hundred men who wore the black beret of Company E, 75th Infantry Rangers, United States Army, Vietnam.

"I'm Sgt. Frost and you are on my team. Get your shit together. We have a mission tomorrow morning."

It was January so the Delta along the Mekong River was hot and dry. In January 1969, it was also especially dangerous for American and Viet Cong soldiers alike.

Sgt. Frost's welcome followed the company commander's equally direct orientation for six replacements who had arrived at Company E that morning.

"Welcome to Vietnam. Four LRRP's were killed last week," the Captain began. "There will be a memorial service here this afternoon at 1400 hours. Be there. This is a volunteer outfit. If you don't want to be a LRRP, you are free to leave now. No hard feelings 'cause we're better off without you. My driver will take you to 9th Division Headquarters and they'll assign you to one of the line companies. Those of you who are staying, let me introduce your team leader." The orientation and in-processing was complete. Sgt. Frost took over.

Sgt. Herbert Frost was an old guy, a lifer, second tour in Vietnam, E-6, 31 years old-more or less. There were three categories of guys in Company E: LRRP's, Lifers and Officers. Everyone arriving for the first time in Vietnam, except lifers, was a cherry. It didn't matter if you were 18 or 22 or 25, it didn't matter if you had significant military training such as ROTC and Ranger. You were young and a cherry. Then, without ceremony, after three weeks with the LRRP's, if you hadn't been blown away, you were no longer young. That's just the way it was.

Getting killed in Vietnam, at least among ground soldiers, seemed mostly accidental. You got in position to be killed because you lost the lottery in demographics or military assignments. The cherry E-4, drafted four months earlier, involuntarily sent to Vietnam and now assigned to the LRRP's couldn't believe his bad luck. LRRP's reportedly ate snakes and ravaged the countryside. LRRP's were dirty, profane and reckless. Hardly the image one wanted on a future resume. From a surreal stage of swirling reddish brown dirt, Frost spoke with the confidence of an actor in a long running one-man show. The cherry stayed.

Frost had re-upped with the Army for six more years at the end of his first enlistment so he was going for 20 years, for the duration. None of the LRRP's re-upped, except lifers like Frost and officers. Some LRRP's had initially enlisted either out of patriotism, foolishness or to avoid going to reform school; a few were draftees. Several volunteered for Vietnam, a few were back in Vietnam for a second tour, but if a

LRRP planned to become "career" Army, i.e., a lifer, you kept that quiet. Basic LRRP theology said the Army sucked and that philosophy kept one from going crazy because, at the bottom, nothing about the war seemed to make sense anyway. The LRRP's considered a lifer a loser. Being a lifer implied one had no other options available. Every LRRP had his own stories about back home: about family, friends, lovers, opportunities, dreams and a future. These were mostly fantasy, but never disputed because, compared to a lifer's world, the preference was obvious.

Like other lifers, Frost had made his peace with the non-commissioned bureaucracy, with the Army's way of business and with the officer structure. He understood why the officers needed separate quarters, clubs and shitters from the LRRPs. He particularly understood this better than the LRRP's because E-6, E-7's and E-8's frequently received a third set of similar accommodations and got special privileges at the NCO club. Frost understood the value of being part of the senior noncom fraternity that could acquire and trade huge quantities of the most important war fighting staples such as steaks, fresh fruits, camouflage fatigues, hard liquor, jeeps and trucks without cash, requisition forms or other red tape.

The E-6 and the E-7 noncoms held the unit together in ways that neither the officers nor LRRPs could do. The officers held higher rank, but the E-6 and E-7, particularly in a combat unit, made things happen or not. The officers could issue orders. The E-6's were buffers, they made sure the LRRPs did work necessary to meet minimum requirements and those other tasks that actually promoted the health and safety of the unit. When the E-6 wanted a jeep or a private shitter, the wise officer figured out a way to let that happen. The LRRP's observed all this, bitched about everything and talked incessantly about how short (days left in Vietnam) they were.

Frost had his own jeep just like the company commander. Company E's authorization was three vehicles since the company had about 120 assigned personnel. On any given day 25 percent were in the field, an equal number on stand down from the previous day's mission and another quarter preparing for the next operation. No one worried about the balance; they would show up when needed. In fact, Company E's motor pool consisted, more or less, of 15 jeeps and trucks. No one questioned the number, why or how; it could have been twenty or ten. When Co. E ran short or the vehicles stopped working, the lifers always had plenty of options for replacements. Camouflage fatigues, available only to "elite" units like the LRRP's and Special Forces were a particularly popular soft currency. Likewise the LRRP's sometimes had access to special weapons or experimental sensing equipment. Collocation on the huge Dong Tam base with the regular 9th Division provided the LRRP's unlimited trading opportunities.

There was another E-6 named Pierre. He wasn't 20 and was on his second Vietnam tour. His pedigree arose from Louisiana or one of the other southern states where tracking critters in the woods was a profession learned early. No one called Pierre a lifer, but, like Frost, he commanded unquestioned combat respect from the LRRP's and the officers. Pierre ran one of the six man teams and cultivated the image of getting great satisfaction from engaging the Viet Cong. He had a sense for where contact could be made and went out of his way not to avoid it. Less adventuresome LRRP's tended to self-select out of his team.

It wasn't the age difference that made Pierre young and Frost old. They represented different generations of soldiers. Frost had the perspective of WW2 and Korean wars. He believed America was in Vietnam for some good reason even if it was beyond his ability to articulate it. Frost believed that when enough gooks were killed, America won.

By contrast, as a child of the 60's, Pierre saw life, including Vietnam, like a series of Disneyland attractions; this thrilling and dangerous ride should be enjoyed for as long as it lasted and then move on to the next. Frost drank copious amounts of beer with the LRRP's and became overbearingly loud without forfeiting the respect and necessary discipline of his team. Pierre smoked a stash with the LRRP's, joked and got mellow without forfeiting the respect and necessary discipline of his team.

Frost entertained small groups of young LRRP's with ribald songs and enriched tales of personal recklessness and debauchery. Under the proper smoking circumstances, Pierre offered rambling, elaborate, enriched descriptions of hairied runs for life from the VC after botched ambushes. After Pierre and Frost went back to the States, we never heard from them again.

Frost was the senior of twelve LRRP team leaders. Each team had five other members plus the team leader. In Vietnam's Delta, along the Mekong River, the LRRP teams conducted recon, patrol, ambush, stay-behind and quick reaction missions. Ambush and quick reaction missions rarely lasted more than 24 hours. The population density of the Delta limited clandestine patrol and recon missions to 48-72 hours. In contrast, LRRP teams in the depopulated north could be in the field for a week or two without detection. LRRP's in Company E, who had been up north, preferred the civilized Delta paddies and Viet Cong to the northern jungle and North Vietnamese Army.

Most missions initiated with a just-at-dusk helicopter insertion of the team on the edge of a recon area or within walking distance of an ambush site. Never resolved running debates occurred among the LRRP's over the merits of moving at night or setting up in a single location. The "keep moving" advocates asserted that LRRP's could see just as well as the VC at night; in fact, with starlight scopes LRRP's had the advantage. The VC didn't expect GI's to be night movers and would have a difficult time locating a team if one was suspected of being in the area. The counter argument asserted that LRRP movement made too much noise that the VC would certainly pick up. Further, the successful ambush required patience. Just like fishing, sitting and waiting would be rewarded. Finally, no one could do a decent recon in the dark.

Pierre argued for night movement because it kept the LRRP's awake and more alert. This became an especially poignant consideration in early 1969 when a team was overrun and 3 LRRP's killed after setting up in a night base camp. Nevertheless, Frost preferred to hole up after dark. He wanted to wait and listen in silence. The first couple times out with Frost, we took no fire and saw no action. Throughout the night, however, anxiety levels were high because the VC conducted logistics, staging operations after dark. Fighting throughout the area was constant and heavy. Daily casualties were taken among the regular 9th division troops in 1968 and 1969 and virtually every Company E LRRP "earned" at least one Purple Heart. In the ten months, September 1968 through June 1969, fourteen LRRP's, over ten percent of Company E's field LRRP's, were killed in action.

Prior to every mission, Frost arranged to be flown over the area of operation in a small observation helicopter. He identified two to four potential landing zones into which the Huey slicks that ferried the LRRP's could work. Insert zones were open grass fields or rice paddies usually surrounded on two or more sides by treelines.

Approaching the insertion area, the Huey pilot descended to treetop level, bobbing in and out of open areas at maximum speed until he reached the zone selected by Frost. As the helicopters momentarily touched ground, three LRRP's on each side of the chopper jumped off the skids. The slicks immediately skimmed out of the LZ just over the wood-line, making one or more additional touch downs to confuse the VC eyes and ears that all knew were observing the action.

On the ground the LRRP's were momentarily exposed and without cover. Off the skids, the LRRP's hit the ground prone sensing the potential for being in the middle of a planned or spontaneous ambush. Absent hostile fire, they ran, crouched, carrying 30 to 50 pounds of gear, M-16's off safety, toward the first available cover and hiding place. Cobra gunships lurked within quick striking distance if the LZ was hot, but every LRRP knew those marvels of firepower couldn't be in position to launch rockets for a minute or two after getting the distress call. If our best friend, Surprise, was with us, even if the VC caught sight of the insertion, they couldn't organize a hostile welcome in the few minutes it took for the LRRP's to move into a defensible position.

Frost had reviewed the terrain maps and plotted a mid-February patrol. In addition to this being the first anniversary of the '68 Tet offensive, Frost's attitude toward the gooks was especially foul. Too many LRRP's had been killed in the past two months and several other combat hardened LRRP's remained on standdown recovering from injury and trauma. Multiple casualties required an adjustment to team composition including distribution of the "cherries"—those newly assigned to the company—to established teams. Normally no team got more than one cherry because everyone understood that a soldier's reaction to his first firefight could not be predicted. In six man teams, one cherry could reasonably be managed by the other five, even if the cherry disintegrated under fire. But few LRRP's team leaders would accept the risk to the team by the uncertainty of two first mission soldiers.

Frost loaded team "one-six" on the Huey slick and headed west of Dong Tam. The first phase of his three day cat and mouse recon mission called for the team to insert along a woodline within VC dominated country side, sit tight until dark, move silently into a relatively defensible area of open rice paddies and observe and report enemy night movement. A 105-artillery battery and a Cobra gunship crew were on alert should the team get into trouble or targets identified.

Frost carried his own radio adding another 15 pounds to his standard gear. He selected an experienced LRRP as point man and designated an equally trusted LRRP as tail gunner. The former had responsibility to sense and spot potential trouble ahead; observe and avoid booby-trapped areas and set the pace of movement. The tail gunner looked backward, observant of any activity behind the patrol such as a scout fleeing the area or an attempt to attack the team from the rear. Frost walked second, LRRP's with some combat, experience walked third and fifth, the cherry walked fourth. In daylight, the LRRP's maintained a 10-yard minimum separation so one grenade won't kill everybody. Frost asked for little more than alertness, silence and willingness to take direction.

Prior to moving out, Frost checked the gear, primarily the number and types of grenades, ammunition and weapons being carried. In reality, the weapon carried by a seasoned LRRP was primarily personal preference so long as the team had sufficient firepower. A few point men carried shotguns. Some LRRP's liked "over and unders," an M-16 combined with a grenade launcher, others swore by the AK-47. One muscular LRRP insisted on carrying the M-60 machine gun like an assault rifle despite the added combined 40-pound weight of gun and ammunition. A majority of the LRRP's stuck with the lightweight, M-16 on full automatic. However, no LRRP wore the universally derided Army issue flack jacket or a steel pot. These were too hot, too heavy and too noisy. On their heads LRRP's wore floppy hats, black berets, bandanas or nothing at all. All LRRP's, including African-Americans, painted exposed skin with green and black camouflage.

Frost had every intention of drawing fire on this mission and killing some gooks to avenge the dead LRRP's. The helicopter insertion was cold and the team hunkered silently in the cover of tall brush. Several minutes after dark, Frost began moving the team parallel to and just inside a woodline. Every hundred meters the team would halt, crouch, wait and listen. When Frost was satisfied with the silence, the march repeated. Under a cloudless, moonless sky the heavily camouflaged LRRP's were invisible to unaided observation. After an hour Frost turned the team perpendicular to the woodline and moved rapidly and silently in low crouch into the middle of an open rice field. Now 150 meters from the woodline and more than 500 meters from the initial insertion point, the LRRP's lay in a line behind a two-foot high rice paddy dike facing the target wood-line. Frost said simply, "this is where we will stay."

With those instructions, the LRRP's paired up for the night. While the cherry would not sleep, the experienced LRRP's had a routine—in three pairs; one LRRP slept one hour then rotated with the partner.

Nights in the dry season had a particular comfort because the paddy wasn't flooded and the air was warm. Half of the team immediately reclined with the dike as backrest, flipped on the safety of their M-16' and were asleep in 90 seconds. Everyone understood that tomorrow we would be humping for 12 hours through the brush and canals trying to get Charlie stirred up enough shoot at us. We were six mice trying to entice a company or battalion sized VC cat to show its fangs. But this evening's insert had been cold and the night remained silent.

"Incoming! Get Down! Now!" As if such orders were necessary. The thump of a mortar, heard clearly even by the sleeping, is as distinctive as the scent of heavy-duty weed. Instantly, safety's snapped off. The LRRP's were tight against the paddy dike, staring through the night black toward the origin of the thump and awaiting an explosion. Another thump and then another. The first shell exploded on the point where, two hours earlier the LRRP's had inserted and small arms fire raked the same area. Succeeding mortars fell in both directions along the recently traversed woodline, each serving as a marking round for follow-on volleys of AK-47 and machine gun fire.

"Sit tight," Frost whispered the order down the line. "Hold fire." With calm satisfaction, he added, "We fooled the bastards. They don't know where we are and are trying to draw us into showing our position by return fire."

Mortar and AK firing continued. After the initial scare, the cherry peeked above the dike. Each time a mortar marked a spot the VC put heavy lead, interspersed with orange and red tracers on the target. The cherry had never seen a display of horizontal fireworks. He marveled at the uncommon brilliance of bullets, whose sole purpose was death and disablement, against the black sky. Until tonight the cherry had thought there could be no beauty in war. Then he shuddered in the warm, tropical night understanding that just as he had the will and capability to kill, others were equally determined to deal him the same fate.

Frost was stoked. He knew the mission had succeeded regardless of what would happen tomorrow. He had the gooks where he wanted them. Talking softly into his PRC-25 radio to a fellow LRRP manning the base camp command post, Frost reported, "We have contact. Do not need extraction. We are not returning fire. Gooks located at coordinate B-7." (Pre-drawn coded coordinates on the operational map for each mission allowed unencrypted radio conversation about locations.) Frost continued, "Prepare fire mission or dispatch Cobras," thereby granting the option for an artillery or air response. Frost had his team on the ground in a safely concealed position from which he could direct big gun or helicopter fire without endangering the team.

Within 15 minutes Cobra gunships were on station and ready to engage. Another mortar thumped and tracer fire from the VC followed.

"We have location of fire. Was that you one-six?" the Cobra pilot asked.

"Negative. That's your target. Make your run," replied Frost. Nearly instantly the far woodlline exploded in flashes of red, orange, blue and yellow as two Cobras rained rockets and miniguns on the gooks.

"Right on target, one more time," Frost directed. The Cobras repeated their run. Light, explosions, fire painted the night sky. The cherry began to understand why some veterans loved Fourth of July fireworks and others would do anything to avoid them.

"Any more?" asked Cobra One.

"Can you hold in the area for a few minutes?" asked Frost.

"Fuel for fifteen."

"OK. Will let you know if we see any movement or need some help."

Silence after firing is quieter than a baby's breathing. For several minutes the LRRP's didn't whisper. Frost surveyed the wood-lines with the starlight scope. There was no movement. There was no sound.

Frost kept looking. The LRRP's listened and stared into the silent night.

"Cobra One, this is one-six, great job. I think we are done for the night."

"One-six, this is Cobra One. Appreciate the opportunity. If anything else happens, we'll be back. Out."

"You will learn those chopper guys are our best friends," said the LRRP beside the cherry.

"Saddle up and move out." In the misty, gray moments, before the dawn that renewed clarity to the world, Frost didn't offer the LRRP's a "Good Morning, Vietnam." Others would own that line. Frost finished coordinating movements with a line company that would sweep the night's Cobra kill area for VC bodies and their weapons. But he also wanted to insure his LRRP's were well hidden before the mamma-sans, papa-sans or VC had a chance to observe their position. Later Frost asked the cherry, "How did you like last night's action?" A reply was unnecessary. "When we get back to the base, I'll let them know you earned your CIB (combat infantry badge)."

Frost liked to move in the daytime and thereby tempt VC response. Along with Pierre, Frost was an advocate of daylight "hunter-killer missions" involving two or three LRRP teams. These operations were a variation on the cat and mouse tactic but used LRRP teams instead of the regular 9th Division companies to engage the cat. Whether they were tactically effective against the VC wasn't a topic of much discussion, but involvement of up to 18 LRRP's in a single mission represented a major commitment of the company's resources. Although the hunter-killer operations required significantly more planning and coordination than recon or ambush missions, with two respected E-6 team leaders as advocates of H-K's, the company commander tended to be supportive.

Frost and Pierre put one together in early 1969. We were somewhere along the Mekong River moving through dry rice paddies dotted with male depleted villages. We took prisoner a man of military age who Frost determined should be interrogated at headquarters by the intelligence units. None of the LRRP's spoke Vietnamese, except for conversation that could solicit beer and boom-boom. Intermittent support from ARVN combat interpreters got mixed reviews by team leaders who often had no patience with Vietnamese interpreters of limited English. On this particular day, as the teams operated without an interpreter and it was uncertain whether or not the prisoner understood our benign intentions.

After picking up the prisoner during the morning patrol, we continued moving through planted paddies and clusters of hootches. At mid-day, our team set up a security perimeter around several abandoned thatched structures intending to rest and nap prior to the night patrol. I had been with these soldiers a few weeks and involved in enough firefights to be accepted as an independent team member. On duty as a perimeter guard that afternoon, I sat leaning against a five foot haystack watching up and down one of the omnipresent canals that lace the Delta. Frost and the resting LRRP's were in the center of the perimeter with the prisoner. The sun was warm, the shade pleasant, and all calm.

Abruptly, shouting resounded at a level and with intensity suggesting an imminent firefight. LRRP's went scrambling, safety's clicked off. I heard and observed nothing in my area, but a flash of movement on my left evoked a spontaneous reaction never before practiced. In a fraction of a second, I swung my rifle in the direction of the movement, recognized a person not more than five feet away running directly at me, then fired a single shot into his chest. The 5.56 round stopped the man. He nearly fell on me. Immediately other LRRP's surrounded us.

"You OK?"
"Yes."
"Son of a bitch tried to escape."
"Looks like you killed him."
"Good work."

The man moaned. Frost came over.

"You OK?"

"Yes."

The man groaned.

"Hit him right in the heart. You want a cigarette?"

"No."

The man moaned.

"He's a goner. Go over with the other guys. We might get some action since they probably heard the shot."

I moved in shock away from the dying man; away from the last sixty seconds of life and death. Then a .45 pistol fired.

Frost rejoined us.

"Poor bastard was suffering badly and was going to die. He's better off now," Frost declared. "Let's pack up and move out now. They will be coming to get him."

LRRP teams were too small, too light and too fast on the move to include a medic.

Frost used the term "gooks" for all the South Vietnamese population—president to peasant, male and female, young or old. The term was not considered particularly pejorative by most LRRP's, although few showed any interest in the Vietnamese beyond engagements that ended at short haircuts, clean laundry or affordable sex. All of these short term, monetary transactions were designed to meet an immediate need or desire of the LRRP while providing valuable, illegal MPC (US Military Payment Currency) to sustain South Vietnam's black market economy.

By contrast, the Viet Cong and the North Vietnamese were "goddamned gooks". This was intended to be pejorative. Combatants seen by the LRRP's through 1969 in the Delta were almost exclusively Viet Cong. Periodic rumors of NVA in the region ran through the unit. Virtually every such rumor included stories about an NVA Colonel whom no one had ever seen. The Colonel's ghostly presence fueled the LRRP's skepticism about the veracity of American military intelligence. Nevertheless, we all agreed that the NVA were real bad asses and we considered ourselves fortunate to be in the South fighting the VC.

Frost frequently spoke derisively of the GD gooks that, he claimed, would never come out and fight LRRP's. They were afraid, and rightly so, asserted Frost, because every time the LRRP's would kick their butts.

Frost had his team hunkered down one afternoon in a huge, dry, rice paddy getting sporadic fire from the treeline several hundred meters distant. The fire was little more than harassment and the bullets flew high above our heads. There wasn't any immediate danger because the Cobras were on standby and we were sitting behind dikes with at least 200 meters of open field inviting a suicidal VC "assault." The VC were equally safe because we couldn't see them hidden in the treeline and couldn't have hit anyone at that distance without a scope. LRRP's also left combat assaults to the regular infantry companies.

For reasons never explained, Frost was suddenly standing six feet four inches erect on top of a hardened mud dike in the middle of a gray-brown, cracked, bone dry rice paddy and shouting, in English, a crude Goliath challenge toward the woodline:

"You fuckin' gooks."

"You are all chicken shits."

"Come out here and get us."

"We'll blow your fuckin heads off."

Frost sat down. There was no applause. No one had shot at him. But Frost was proud. He hadn't needed a speech writer. Two LRRP's looked at each other. "Crazy fucker," whispered one. The other nodded and stared ahead at the wood-line.

Frost's hatred of the VC was professional. Regardless of the cause or nationality, Frost would have hated any opposing combatant. In each VC casualty, Frost saw a small step toward eventual victory. At another level, Frost may have recognized his life in Vietnam with the LRRP's was as good as it would get for him. So, his afternoon proclamation—raw, racist, and ritualistic—drew on an ethos recited every week in locker rooms across America. Frost had proclaimed this was his game day, his showtime; he entered the mental zones known by competitors, soldiers and lovers when one is invincible and never more alive. Frost was in Vietnam eager to be part of war.

Frost normally held his tongue when the LRRP's bitched about officers. If officers described themselves as gentlemen, strategists and leaders, the LRRP's described them as candy asses and suck-ups. Frost didn't argue with the LRRP's, but preferred that officers tend to base camp chores such as mission coordination or planning, but stay out of the field. If an officer joined a team, the command structure got all screwed up. The officer was nominally in charge but often had limited or no field experience. To the LRRP's, he didn't know jack shit and was dangerous to everyone including himself. The LRRP's relied on their "real" team leader to keep everyone alive and discourage the officer from adventuresome exploits. LRRP's defined successful "officer led missions" as short, devoid of enemy contact and casualty free. Even better was when the officer announced that the team was doing so well that he didn't need to go out with them again.

Officers came to Company E for three reasons: to log credible combat time; to get a Combat Infantry Man's Badge; and to collect combat medals. Since officers were required to spend only six months "in the field," a new one seemed to show every couple months.

Frost had a special contempt for a pudgy, ego driven, Fort Benning trained Ranger named Martin. Lt. Martin tried to be friendly; the LRRP's saw him as just another rank climber. Martin believed he had a mandate to lead; the LRRP's didn't consider themselves leaderless prior to Martin's arrival.

Going into 1969, daytime Search and Destroy missions by 9th Division line companies were being increasingly directed from command helicopters. A battalion commander would establish a helicopter command post several thousand feet above several companies conducting a combat sweep. Since the VC had no capability to counter the helicopter at that altitude, the commander in the sky could visually direct the ground movements. Company commanders on the ground were like football quarterbacks, paid to execute the play called from the press box. Since LRRP missions were intended to be clandestine for as long as possible, Company E had been insulated from this tactic. Then, Lt. Martin arrived.

Lt. Martin liked the concept of daytime operations with LRRP teams executing short duration, hit and run missions. Called Parakeets, four or five lightly armed LRRP's would load into a Huey and, supported by a Cobra gunship, go looking to stir up action. The Huey skimmed the countryside at treetop level trying to draw fire, or dipped lower as it flew along river banks, and would (without a fly-by) touch down to put the LRRP's on the ground for 10 minutes to check out a suspicious hooch or bunker. No effort was made to conceal the presence of the team and Huey. If the VC could be enticed to open fire, so much the better; a Cobra gunship was on station and would respond. LRRP's began to like the Parakeet Missions because they were flying rather than humping the paddies and everyone got back to the compound for the evening.

According to Frost, who told the story during a marathon beer binge, Lt. Martin had taken a team on a Parakeet Mission a couple days earlier. Movement meriting investigation was spotted and the team immediately inserted, but Martin stayed on the chopper. The LRRP's began a cautious patrol and quickly spotted several males in VC black running in the treeline. The Cobra fired rockets and miniguns into the target area. The LRRP's added ground level fire and took some return fire that was readily suppressed by another Cobra run. Adrenaline flowed on the ground and in the air. The size of the VC force was unknown, but solid contact had been made.

"We've got them pinned down," reported the LRRP on the ground. "Can we get a line company on them?"

From 2500 feet Martin surveyed the flooded paddies and lush palm. He couldn't see the individual LRRP's but there weren't any bunkers and the VC didn't hold a very strong defensive position.

"Negative on the line company. You see any more movement?" Martin radioed.

"No."

A few minutes passed.

"Air One-Two (Martin's call sign) here. Have you taken any more fire?"

"Negative. The Cobra did its job but we can't see very far into the wood-line."

"Check it out for bodies and weapons."

"No can do. The grass is tall and the palm is thick. There could be a dozen more laying an ambush in there."

"We have you covered. Move on in. Be careful."

"This doesn't look right."

"OK, we'll put the Cobra on it once more."

Rockets screamed and exploded through the light palm canopy. A fresh Cobra joined the force shredding foliage with the lead hail from two miniguns.

"One-Two, we see three guys running."

"Go after them," ordered Martin.

"If there's three, there are probably more holed up in there."

"The Cobra's flushed them out, I said get after them."

Two LRRP's moved into the wood-line, two others followed. They stopped and listened to the silence. Quietness like snow falling in a mountain wilderness shrouded the team.

In low crouch, the two LRRP's sprinted 30 feet for the cover of the canal embankment. A step short of the canal bank AK-47, fire cut them down.

Silently the blood of two LRRP's ran into the canal.

Frost's voice was simultaneously choked and furious. "Do you know what that son of a bitch Martin did then?"

It was a rhetorical question. No LRRP dared interrupt. Frost could be mean when drunk. He was retelling the story as related to him by the surviving LRRP's to an audience predisposed to dislike Martin.

"The SOB says to the two other guys still on the ground, 'Don't let them get away. Assault. Return fire.'

"He's up there at three thousand feet trying to get the whole team killed. But the other guys had better sense than to listen to that fucker. They just shut the radio off, hugged the ground, and began a slow belly down backwards crawl out of the foliage."

Frost continued, "The dumb son of a bitch ordered the chopper down right where the LRRP's had first penetrated the woodline. Now he's got two dead LRRP's, doesn't know where the others are and is risking a chopper and the pilots in a situation he doesn't have a clue about."

So the chopper sets down, Martin jumps and sees the two surviving LRRP's clear the woodline.

"We're going in to get them," Martin shouted. The LRRP's were in too much shock to do anything but follow.

Frost was enraged, "So two boys are already dead, there's no back up expect the Cobras that have already spent most of their ammo when he takes those two poor, scared bastards right back into the brush. I wish he would have gotten his. It's a miracle they all weren't killed."

Over the hour, Frost had become drunk, depressed and angry.

"And do you know what the asshole was really doing? Do you think he cared about the LRRP's? No. He had already gotten two killed and now he was willing to risk the other two for a second time. Three of them walking right back to where they had just gotten ambushed. All the asshole could think about was being written up as fuckin' hero and getting his medal. He should be court martialed for murder."

Two weeks later in a ceremony attended only by those LRRP's ordered to be there, Lt. Martin received the Silver Star. Lt. Martin was cited for uncommon heroism in risking his life to save two LRRP's and to recover the remains of two LRRP's killed in action. To be fully accurate, as every LRRP knew, the citation should have also stated that not a single shot was fired the entire time Martin was on the ground that day.

The last time I saw Frost was in late June. The team was called unexpectedly for a mission the day that I was scheduled to leave for R&R in Hong Kong. Frost said, "No big deal. I'll get one of the other guys to go. It's a one day operation anyway."

By then the whole war in the Delta had taken a different direction. Nixon had ordered the pullout of some of the 9th Division as the first step in his policy of turning the war over the Vietnamese. The Dong Tam base would be occupied by the ARVN in July and any remaining US units, including Company E, relocated. Several LRRP's had been interviewed a few days earlier by one of the US news networks. To the momentary dismay of some of the 9th Division brass, the LRRP's openly questioned the wisdom of the pullout, asserting that their experience suggested the war in the Delta was more intense than ever. What the LRRP's saw night after night on the ground was the opposite of the official line that the Viet Cong in the South had been weakened, contained-even defeated. At the same time most LRRP's would have been happy to be among the units being "brought home."

I expected to rejoin Frost's team when I returned from Hong Kong, but he, unexpectedly, had been sent back in the States. The LRRP's had already reallocated the gear he left behind—poncho liners, knives, side arms, wool socks—according to the "first come, first get" policy. Another E-6 had moved into Frost's private room. I had six months in country and became a team leader inheriting several members of Frost's team.

Although Frost was such a dominant figure in the company, his departure didn't seem to leave much of an operational hole. The unit was designed to accommodate unplanned turnover because all of us lived with the understanding that anyone could be gone the next day. There was probably some kind of farewell for Frost, but it must have occurred before I returned from Hong Kong. I thought about Frost more than I thought about other departed E-6's not because I particularly liked or knew him well, but because he seemed more the prototype of the core Army NCO's than others. For Frost, his image and his rank were inextricably intertwined. He carried out his duties well enough. He didn't put people in greater danger than what he was willing to accept. He knew his job, didn't complain, and let others know what needed to be done. He also needed to be seen as larger than life, as more than another lifer E-6. He partially achieved that. Thirteen years after he went back to the States, Herbert Frost's name, along with 55,000 others, was chiseled on a black marble wall that stands in the afternoon shadow of the Lincoln Memorial in Washington, DC.

On June 21, Frost had taken a single round in the heart. Since LRRP's travel light and fast, Frost had no medic to treat him. He died in a rice paddy, near an abandoned thatched hooch. None of the LRRP's could say for sure whether it was a VC or an American bullet. Nor was anyone quite certain whether or not Frost was the intended target. No one tried very hard to determine the details of Frost's death. It didn't seem to matter. And we had a mission in the morning.

Kill Them All

by Jack Bick

"Damn gook," exclaimed the bus driver as he swerved to miss a family of four balancing on and riding a bicycle. So, this was Vietnam; a disorganized shambles of bicycles, rickshaws, Vespa motorcycles, small cars, busses and military "deuce and a halfs". My first thoughts were of the dangers of merely driving in this country and how animal-like these people were.

The streets were dirty with heavy dust and trash. Laundry hung from every window and balcony. The buildings were in disrepair or were makeshift in nature. There wasn't a fence or piece of wood in sight that didn't need painting. The gutters of the streets ran with sewage or were stained by it. I remembered the words of our training sergeant back at Fort Riley, Kansas, "These gooks are animals with little regard for human life—theirs or yours." That five days of training for Vietnam was scarcely enough, but I remember every word because my life did depend on it. With a degree in journalism I went directly from basic training to a duty station.

Assigning me to something I knew was probably a momentary lapse on the Army's part. However, the powers that be came through in true army form by sending me to Fort Riley where there was no need for a journalist, so I became a morning report clerk. Once I was reassigned to Vietnam, the five days of training amongst the oak trees in Kansas was all that was available.

Arriving in DongTam, the headquarters for the Ninth Division, I experienced more evidence of the less than human nature of our enemy. Up close, the people were dirtier than the surroundings. Their hair was matted down by dirt. Their teeth were shades of yellow and brown, a combination of poor diet and chewing on leachy betel nuts and other unsavory substances.

A trip outside the compound offered more evidence of subhuman existence. We headed north on Highway One toward Saigon. An overturned garbage truck left the people ravaging through the stink and slime, sometimes eating what they found right there knee deep in slop. "How could human beings live like this," I wondered?

Further up the road we encountered a roadside stop for the civilian busses. This was not a place of restaurants, gas stations, restrooms and motels. It was the proverbial wide spot in the road where the locals gathered to board the bus. Vendors sold peeled pineapples on a stick, peanuts in a cone of white or pink paper and other foods. The riders, male and female, descended into the ditch along the side of the road to squat and relieve themselves much like dogs or cats.

Passengers were packed to overflowing while still others braved the ride on top of the bus. The busses traveled at breakneck speeds along the narrow highway taking daredevil chances to pass any vehicle that moved slower. The only deference to safety, was a person stationed on the back of the bus to signal the driver when it was safe to pull back into the proper lane after a pass. The real test to nerves came when two of these vehicles had to pass in opposite directions on this narrow roadway. While Highway One was the major artery running south out of Saigon into the Mekong Delta, it was nothing more than a narrow two lane humpback road.

The most important human faculty was impossible to bring to bear—communication. They spoke a sing-song language that was delivered in squeaky tones and fast bursts. Many sounds repeated in succession made it more like gibberish than a language. These people had not developed a language; how could we ever expect them to be sanitary and productive?

Like animals they slept whenever and wherever they got tired, in the heat of the afternoon, instead of buckling down to the task at hand, they layed down in hallways, in any shady spot, or even in a hammock under a truck to sleep.

It was no problem to hunt these creatures in the jungle—these dirty, little uneducated creatures.

And hunt them we did. We hunted them with large units of line troopers. We hunted them with small units of Rangers. We employed the most modern equipment known to man. We attacked from the air, the water and the ground. We used weapons of destruction and psychological weapons to make them "chou hoi"—surrender.

As a journalist for the army, officially called the public information office, I had liberties unavailable to few of the soldiers around me. In the Ninth Division we wore no rank. We obviously were not officers, but those of us working in the field with the line units did not have to visually declare rank on our uniforms.

The units we were in were not in our chain of command. Our superiors were back in the base camp, Dong Tam. Their absence combined with the absence of rank were constant irritations to the First Sergeants of the line unit. While the superiors in the line unit could not directly order us around, it was smart to follow their directives unless it was not in the best interest of doing our job.

Basically we were charged with covering the activities of our unit. These stories would be published in "Stars and Stripes" which was a daily publication, "The Old Reliable" which was a weekly, or other publications within the army's control. We were also expected to shoot two rolls of film in the field and do a minimum of ten "hometowners" per week which were sent to the soldier's hometown newspapers. My unit was the 3rd Battalion, 60th Infantry, 9th Infantry Division.

Covering this unit was easy because they operated in the Mekong Delta and made considerable contact with the enemy every day. If we couldn't flush them out we would sniff them out, with helicopters that carried devices that could detect ammonia trails that remain in the air when a group of humans move through. We could move in on a target from the air, on boats and on the ground.

Within three weeks of my assignment, my stories appeared on the front page of "Stars and Stripes" which made the battalion commander very happy. You can imagine how happy he was when our news was repeated over the next few weeks. I was his public relations man and that gave me even more liberty to go on the missions I wanted and to move about freely.

The battalion commander was open to my requests to fly on the "sniffer" missions or the "psyops" leaflet drops or three day ops on the communications boats or to ride along with the Navy swift boats. The lieutenant colonel and I had an undeclared bond to keep each other happy.

On many occasions I participated in Ranger operations with the blessing of the battalion commander. One such mission was an early morning helicopter insertion on Feb. 21, 1969. I had my choice of a mission with a line unit of up to 100 soldiers, or this "hunter-killer" mission with 18 Rangers.

There wasn't a cloud in the sky as the three huey helicopters flew by the predetermined landing zone at 5000 feet. Sergeant Frost gave the signal and we were on the way in, three on each side, sitting with out feet out of the open door. As we approached the ground, we scooted forward to stand on the skids in order to jump off without the helicopter actually touching down.

This was the moment of truth when we were the most vulnerable hanging there in the air. The feeling of being hot on the outside and cold on the inside came over me. Every one of my senses seemed to peak. The sounds of the blades were deafening, the feel of my uniform against my skin almost hurt, the smell of the moist rice paddy hit me like smelling salts. It seemed that I could see every leaf on the trees of the wood-line in front of us.

The LZ was cold, no enemy fire. I could breathe again. Sergeant Frost wanted us to stay low and still for a few minutes while he visually reconned the area. This was a cross shaped rice paddy with each leg less than a mile in length. Heavy jungle surrounded us on all sides. Each leg of the cross was approximately 150 yards wide.

We were positioned closer to the woodline on the right. This was a "hunter-killer" mission, so Frost wanted to decide where to send in the hunter team of six men while the killer team set up. Frost made his decision and sent the hunter team into the wood-line. He came over to me: "We're going to get you into a firefight before we fly out of here tomorrow. I promise you." I nodded approval even though he didn't have to try so hard on my account.

I had been with this unit since late December and had never been in a real firefight. There were several occasions when we were fired upon or where we killed some of the enemy, but not a real firefight with a consistent exchange of fire.

As the killer teams headed to the edge of the tree line to set up, my senses were still on full alert. A 35mm camera was slung to my back and my M-16 in front at full ready.

Dikes running through the rice paddy were designed to hold water during the rainy season and to allow for walking trails above the level of the mud. These dikes had vegetation growing on them meaning that the locals did not walk on them because they were booby trapped. The rice paddies were still wet but not full of water.

While we did capture one local, he was killed as he tried to escape. Otherwise the day and the night that followed were rather uneventful. Sergeant Frost was not happy. He wanted a body count and a real firefight for me. Sergeant Frost and I had become friends. This was his second tour of Nam. He said he didn't want to get out of the Army because his father-in-law would put him to work in the insurance business.

Sergeant Frost was educated and ruggedly handsome with a bushy mustache. He walked with a confidence that showed he was comfortable doing what he was doing-"wasting gooks" in his words.

In desperation he called for extraction in one hour. The following events took about 30-40 minutes but even today they flash before me as if they only took a few minutes.

It was the anniversary of my grandfather's birthday, I prayed that I did not join him in heaven that day. Sergeant Frost took us into the rice paddy right down the middle between two heavy woodlines. Some of the Rangers thought it was reckless but they knew Sergeant Frost wasn't going to leave without tempting the gooks to come out and fight.

The first rounds aimed high and came from the wood-line to the right. This gave us time to get to the dike for cover before the gooks could control their AK-47s and direct the rounds lower.

"Take cover"..."Get down"..."Don't get too close.", shouted several of the Rangers.

Making sure my camera was slung to the back, I hit the ground. We all started firing at the wood-line with no distinct target in mind, just gain fire superiority. A few of the men with grenade launchers started pumping them into the trees as well. Frost was calling for air support on the radio. About the time Yates got the M-60 going, I noticed that some rounds were coming from behind me and landing with a "thump" in the mud in front of me. About the time that I realized we were taking fire from both sides, Frost yelled for every other man to jump to the other side of the dike. Rather than expose myself to more risk, I rolled over the dike and started hitting the other wood-line with my weapon on full automatic. I had gone through three clips by the time I heard someone yell, "Where the fuck are those gun ships?"

Frost was on the radio again letting the air support know that we were receiving fire from both sides. We, in turn, were putting a lot of lead into both tree-lines with M-16s, grenade launchers and machine guns. The sound was intense and so was the experience.

As we received less fire, I surmised that the gooks were running out of ammo, or they were headed deeper into the jungle for cover, or we had killed some of them. The true answer became academic since we didn't go in to count the bodies.

The air support arrived and the fire power directed into those wood-lines left little chance for anything still there to survive. First in were the LOHs, Light Observation Helicopters, with mini-guns mounted on the front. Leaves, then branches, then the tops of trees began to fall to the ground. Next, our Hueys arrived and the door gunners worked on the tree-line close to the ground. First one side, then the other, trying to eliminate anyone one on the ground who might shoot while we boarded the choppers.

Meanwhile on the ground, we felt the glow of victory. "Let me shoot the grenade launcher," I asked of the man next to me. He gladly handed it to me. To every one's glee, I put the round so high that it went over the tree-line. "Hey, they are in retreat, I had to shoot for the long distance," I proclaimed.

The Hueys came in fast and we had but a split second to climb aboard before the pilot lifted off. As soon as we were on, the door gunners opened up with the M-60s and we a knelt in the doorways firing into the vegetation. We worked over one wood-line, then the other, and just as quick the jets came in with more fire power and bombs. If the gooks were to survive that kind of fire, they were going to have to be fast runners or deep underground.

As time went on, we learned that the gooks were good at quick hits, swift movement and surviving underground. As much as you hated Charlie, as we called the Viet Cong, you also developed a respect for their inner strength and tenacity.

These facts of survival made many of the troops want to kill the enemy even more. They hunted these creatures with a real depth of purpose and design. When they killed the enemy, it wasn't just what a soldier was required to do, it was something deeper. Our soldiers would take the enemy's possessions such as wallets, photos and jewelry to revel in the kill, to have a trophy like someone who hunts deer rather than humans.

It even drove some to riddle the dead bodies with bullets until there was nothing left but a pile of bloody meat. Others would dismember the dead cutting off fingers, ears or heads. The worst that I observed was the cutting of the throat of an enemy soldier, wounded, but still very much alive.

This is not difficult to understand when you realize how we dehumanize our enemies. That is what allows one human being to kill another human being. The Germans did it to the Jews, we did it to the Vietnamese and today it is done to the innocent unborn in the name of women's rights.

Not all my adventures included killing the enemy. On several occasions we would secure a village and bring in the doctors and the medics to minister to the sick and to give shots to the children so that if they survived the gun fire, disease would not kill them. In the children you could see the humanity of the Vietnamese people and you had to acknowledge it.

Their children were no different than our children. Give them a ball or a tricycle and they would play. Build them a slide and they would climb up and slide down in glee.

Few of the combat troops were ever given the chance to see the children play in these villages. This was fortuitous since it might have taken the fight out of them if they realized that we were hunting human beings just like ourselves. Survival required us to see them as the enemy, as less than human.

Kodak Moments

by Bob Wallace

At the Travis Air Force Base Exchange camera counter, I bought the smallest Kodak on display for fifteen dollars. It seemed like a good idea because I had never been to Vietnam and the folks at home always enjoyed snapshots. Actually, I had never been outside the United States, nor had either of my parents. So I loaded up with half a dozen extra rolls of film because I expected to take quite a few pictures and didn't know if Kodak film would be available over there.

Until arrival at Travis, a sense of denial about the whole Vietnam thing clouded my reality. Particularly with the 1968 election of Nixon and his "secret plan" for ending the war, my optimism soared. This little war would be over soon and my involuntary military service would end after 24 months in Texas or Alabama. Except now the cycle of unit movements, waiting, moving, waiting, and boarding calls at Travis began to burn off the fog of unreality.

The World Airways 707 we boarded had been converted to six abreast, 40 rows of troop seating. It would be a through flight to Saigon with refueling stops in Alaska and Japan—two other places I would see for the first time in the next twenty-four hours. Assigned to a window seat, I was able to take a couple pictures of the 707's wing sitting on a background of cotton fluff clouds. Alaska is rather cold in January so my only picture there consisted of the outside of the terminal. In Japan, we felt the tiredness that comes from trans-pacific flights, despite excellent attention by flight attendants, and grouped like drifters on the floor, benches and chairs, wherever we could find space as we awaited the final leg.

Over the next twelve months my artistic skills as a photographer did not improve. But that little camera, by accident, became as close a companion as my M-16. When we drew the standard web gear, a variety of pockets or carrying cases were available to attach to the gear. A small five by two by one and a half inch case with an end snap opening fit on the web's vertical shoulder strap. The Kodak nestled comfortably into the case with enough room to be easily removed and reinserted. It was wonderful to see a plan come together. So throughout 1969, the Kodak went on more than 100 combat missions, available whenever wanted and well protected from rain, dirt and damage by a durable canvas pouch that probably had a specific military use when designed.

The images of Vietnam captured thus by the Kodak are on slides and black & white and color prints. They reside in a trunk with other Vietnam era memorabilia that hasn't been looked at in a decade or two. They are ill captioned and mostly faded. Many of the faces I could no longer identify nor would I know the locations of most of the countryside scenes. At the time, the images seemed to have enormous significance; today no one would pay good cash for any of them and I do not receive serious requests for viewing by family or friends. They are the physical counterparts of another set of snapshots that endure in my memory. The latter are so imprinted on mind that any mention of Vietnam immediately loads and flashes that equally real collection of slides across my imagination. These mental photographs capture images of combat and daily routines of 1969 life with the 9th Infantry Division's Company E, 75th Infantry Rangers.

Title: Culture Shock
Setting: Evening near dusk

Location: Tan Son Nhut Air Force Base
Date: January 1969

All the vehicles looked miniaturized, beat up and carried funny sounding Japanese and Korean names. Each was loaded with an unbelievable number of remarkably small people. We were somewhere near an entry gate to Tan Son Nhut just after arriving from the World flight, awaiting transportation to a reception post. As a Kansas farmer, I knew a world of fairly sizable trucks that hauled grain, livestock and building materials. People rode in cars.

Here, hundreds of Vietnamese who worked along side Americans during the day crowded, pushed and jostled for space on a menagerie of pickups, trucks, buses, and mopeds. Loading these vehicles could be compared to '60's college pranks of getting the maximum number of kids into telephone booths or in a Volkswagen Beetle. Except this wasn't for fun and the participants weren't drinking. Six or more sat in a truck cab. Twenty-five stood, sat or held on in an open bed of small pickups. Those unable to get inside or on top of a bus found a place for one foot on a bumper and a handgrip on an open window and dangled in suspension above the roadway.

On one occasion, I took a short "civilian" local bus ride between two bases. Every element of daily Vietnam transportation life—the heat, humidity, dust, jarring roads, frequent stops, hard seating and traffic chaos—was part of the trip, except this American soldier found that he had a seat to himself. Never mind that the 80 or so other passengers were jammed back to chest, the American got space. I did not understand if this was from fear or loathing, from respect or courtesy, or possibly Vietnamese shock at seeing a lone American in the middle of their daily routine. Subsequently our commanding officer let me know with clear language that the little ride had been stupid, dangerous, unauthorized and was not to be repeated.

Title: The Business of War
Setting: Bright sun

Location: Dong Tam Base
Date: February 1969

The docks at Dong Tam, a base along the Mekong River fifty or so kilometers south of Saigon, could have been dedicated to Coca-Cola and Bud. If World War II soldiers marched on their stomachs, the 9th Division must have survived on liquids. Lines and stacks of pallets of Budweiser, Coca-Cola and their numerous competitors so dominated the Dong Tam dock transit area that one could wonder if beverage cans were the weapon of choice. Vietnam's 24 hour per day outdoor oven had translated into, not profits for suppliers of war materials, but for America's beverage and refrigerator manufacturers. The folk song asked, "Where have all the flowers gone?", I still wonder what happened to all those millions of aluminum cans.

Title: Reality
Setting: Midday Shade
Location: Mekong River
Date: March 1969

By late March, I had been in Vietnam over two months but not reconciled to the fate of being a combat ranger. The mail room or company clerk represented more attractive assignments. I just couldn't figure out how to arrange that. In general I was mad at the government for drafting me and for not winning the war earlier. I was mad at the Army for sending me to Vietnam instead of Germany. I wasn't very happy with God, either, for allowing all this to happen. So along with a rotten attitude, I would do the minimum to get out of the Vietnam prison as soon and as safely as possible. By contrast, Sgt. Newman was having the time of his life.

How Newman and I became friends isn't clear. We arrived as replacements for Company E on the same day in January. Newman had been in Vietnam a couple years earlier with the 82nd and volunteered a second tour with the Ranger unit. He was jump qualified, 20 years old and a college drop out. At twenty-four I was the oldest person in the Company, (outside of the career soldiers), and, with a Masters Degree, one of the most "educated." Newman came from a large Catholic urban family living in a city, my small Baptist family lived on a farm. Nevertheless some common interests seemed to exist and friendship grew as we spent down time together between missions.

Newman had affection for the M-60 machine gun. On our six man teams, the M-60 gave a high level of confidence to withstand a firefight and it provided a deadly effective weapon for close in ambush. The weight of the gun wasn't an issue so long as someone wanted to carry the extra weight, but the ammunition was a problem. Since a machine gun consumed ammunition at a faster rate than the assault rifles and the M-60 ammo was larger and heavier than the M-16 round, someone other than the gunner must also be willing to carry a heavier load. After Newman and I had become friends, we were assigned to the same team and on occasion I would "volunteer" to be his ammo bearer.

We sat back to back under a coconut tree one afternoon waiting for nightfall and movement to an ambush point. I offered another round of grousing about the circumstances of our being in this nasty war focusing exclusively on the personal unfairness of it all. Newman wasn't amused or especially charitable. Without a tape recorder, the words may not be exact, but the content is accurate.

"You whine and bitch. You're not doing yourself or me any good. You're here. I'm here. And like it or not we're probably here until next January unless one of us gets shot. You probably don't want that."

He continued, "What's so bad anyway? These are good guys to be around. We work together. We look out for each other. The chopper pilots will get us out if we run into shit. You've got a bunk to sleep in with a roof and an electric fan. We've got good weapons. We aren't hassled, just have to hump the paddies and stay alert. The weather is pretty good, not cold like Korea. There's plenty to eat. We've got weights to lift, books to read and cold beer. You get letters and packages from home and from Mary Margaret. Are you going to make yourself miserable and not have any friends for the next nine months? Think about it."

A lot of mental fog lifted that afternoon. Circumstances and events weren't changed at all, but things sure looked different. It was an uneventful afternoon that totally transformed the tour. Amazing was how much I began to like Vietnam, the people and the culture. The countryside had a new beauty and the war became an event of great tragedy for all involved. Unwanted and unplanned conditions frequently intrude on our planned lives. In such circumstances, I've thought often about Newman's sermon that, while devoid of scriptural quotations, must have been inspired by The Old Testament prophet, Jeremiah, chapter 29.

Title: Paradise
Setting: Bright Sunlight
Location: Nha Trang
Date: April 1969

The men of Company E, 75th Rangers, wore black berets and traced their military lineage to Merrill's Marauders of World War II fame. The myth of this heritage and that of a "Ranger" seeped into the psychology of the unit. Some, like myself, however, drafted in 1967 and 1968, came into the Army as pure infantry replacements and had neither volunteered for an "elite" fighting unit nor had any of the specialized training of the true "Ranger." The latter deficiency could be partially addressed by attending a three-week Special Forces led "Recondo" course near Nha Trang, on South Vietnam's east central coast.

Recondo School taught combat reconnaissance tactics for small recon teams and pushed the physical limits of the trainees. Graduation required completion of a 7 mile run with full combat gear under 90 minutes and a five-day live recon operation in the mountains of the region. Doing the 7 mile run was a terrific confidence builder and the recon operation was an endurance hike without contact or enemy sighting. However neither core activity left as vivid a memory as the free afternoon on the beach.

A couple weeks into the training we were ferried to a nearby offshore island with no mission other than to enjoy the ocean and the beach. The sight stunned me. A broad beach of the whitest sand stretched for an indefinite distance kissed by the gentlest of waves from an ocean with water so clear that standing chest depth, you could see your toes. I had never imagined such beauty and thought how, absent the war, I was standing in the kind of South Sea Paradise that drew 16th century explorers to this distant world.

Title: Tea Time
Setting: Dim Indoors
Location: Saigon
Date: May 1969

"GI, You buy me tea?"

The U.S. Army approved certain bars and steak houses for enlisted men in Saigon. The war in the Delta seemed quite distant although the sandbags at the entrance to this particular establishment reminded one that the city lived in fear as well. The air conditioning worked exceptionally well. The floors were carpeted, the décor upscale, the furnishings well kept and the outside noise had been abated by acoustic treatment. Several Vietnamese hostesses were working the tables but, for a first time visitor, in a curious manner. Rather than continually making the rounds from table to table, they would frequently serve an order and then snuggle up to the customer for what seemed to be extended conversation. After a period of observation, I concluded this was not a difficult industry to understand. Upon first encounter, the rules and procedures were much different than in the unregulated "bars" outside the gates of bases like Dong Tam. This was the world of Saigon tea.

With plenty of American MPC (military payment currency) which could be converted to dollars or exchanged at inflated rates on the black market, a comfortable, cool environment, relative safety and opportunity for female companionship, the LRRP found it difficult to refuse to buy the lady a tea. The fact that the tea was half the cost of a beer made the answer even easier. Quickly, however, it became apparent that the young lady, as fascinated as she might be with her new companion, had an insatiable addiction to the tea. In fact, she required replenishment about every ten minutes. Without that sustained flow of tea, the lady found it necessary to resume her role as waitress and hostess as she greeted new arrivals with the friendliness and open attraction that, with tea, had been the heart of the just concluded tete-a-tete.

Nevertheless, one did not need to be lonely for long, because within a few minutes, another of the hostesses, would sit down, touch softly and whisper, "GI, you buy me tea?" In the tea room, opportunity knocked more than once throughout the evening. It continued until closing after which some of the tea girls signaled availability for extended relationships.

Title: The Throne
Setting: Indoors Flash
Location: Hong Kong
Date: June 1969

Survive 6 months "in country" and you get five days R&R (rest and relaxation) at a place of your choice, so long as the quota for that location isn't already filled. Among the approved locations were Hawaii, Japan, Australia, Thailand and Hong Kong. The married guys mostly went to Hawaii to be with their wives. Lots of the single guys went to Bangkok because it had a reputation for beautiful and available women. I went to Hong Kong because it sounded exotic and I wanted to see China.

Upon arrival we immediately received the "good behavior: you are an example for America and the US Army, don't be obnoxious; avoid becoming criminally drunk, try not to catch STD's" (sexually transmitted disorders), briefing. We checked into a decent hotel. Within minutes, I discovered that no facility had ever been more welcome than the private bath. The porcelain shone, hot and cold water ran on command; the shower's controlled pressure and water temperature regulator were marvelous. But nothing surpassed the flush toilet and its smooth, contoured seat. For six months, the daily toilet facilities had been slit latrines, or a hole in a flat pine board suspended over a half 55 gallon drum or squatting in the rice paddies. I sat for a long time on that commode relishing the comforts of 20th century technology applied to the necessities of life.

Title: Soda Fountain
Setting: Full Sunlight
Location: Highway South of Saigon
Date: July 1969

A single paved two lane highway ran south from Saigon to My Tho and into the Delta. At every intersection with a major foot trail or a vehicle track, little one and two stool food and drink stands sprang up. Most offered bottled soft drinks and "33" beer, along with bread, noodles and broth. These were Vietnam's fast food way-stations for travelers who, whether walking or riding, were all hot, hungry and thirsty. The stands consisted of a weathered wooden serving table two or three feet long. Up scale competitors offered outdoors seating on stool or chair with limited, premium seating under a beach umbrella. All permitted smoking. The broth and noodles were in constant preparation in a black pot over an open fire of twigs that smoldered throughout the day. Like the stature of the South Vietnamese, the "furnishings" appeared small, undersized, almost frail to an American used to stainless steel diners and Formica countertops. The local Vietnamese police and military personnel were prominent among the clientele. The stands opened at daybreak, closed at sunset. All activity in the Delta's countryside, except for American patrols and Viet Cong logistics movements, ceased when darkness fell.

Coke, a universally known word, dominated the beverage sales. While no GI disputed the "fact" that Coke bottled in Asia tasted inferior to that in the US, the convenience of a clearly understood communication, "Give me a Coke," outweighed the hassle of trying to express another preference. That determined, circumstances now required the customer make other choices as well. Will the Coke be served room temperature or chilled? Will it be in a glass or drunk from the bottle? Sometimes chilled Coke was not an option because ice in the Delta came dearly. Somebody, somewhere did make ice and got it distributed in small quantities through the private economy. However, the absence of electric power and refrigeration except on military bases and in selected parts of primary cities limited its availability. As a result, the wayside stand offering chilled Coke had a couple chunks of ice in a box or bucket with the Coke sitting on top of the ice. Chilled meant anything lower than the outdoor temperature.

The proprietor generally had a few glasses for serving Coke or beer. These ranged in size from 4 ounce juice glasses to 16 ounce tumblers of every shape imaginable. After use, the glasses were rinsed in a small plastic (often green) pan holding an inch or two of water. The wash water had a daylong shelf life. This influenced American customers to drink directly from the bottle. All beverages were consumed on site and the bottle, due to its value, returned. The stands were all operated by women of indeterminate age, some with children playing along side.

The ritual of ice captured my attention. Rare commodities must be conserved and ice was such a commodity. If one wanted a drink colder than "chilled," the Coke could be served with ice. This might cost another ten cents. A small chunk of ice would be chipped by hand from the larger block, then placed in a glass. Coke was poured. Since a single chunk of ice in a glass does not melt quickly, when the drink was finished, the ice was pretty well intact. The proprietor put the glass and ice into the wash pan, retrieved the ice and returned it to the other container. The next customer ordering Coke with ice likely got the recycled chunk of ice, a pattern that continued until the ice had completely melted. For most GI's who observed the ritual, the temperature of slightly chilled Coke served in the bottle became fully acceptable.

Title: Medavac
Setting: Hazy Sunlight
Location: Vietnam Delta
Date: August 1969

The unexpected explosion wasn't especially loud but it was too close. There was no accompanying gunfire, just an unintelligible jumble of yelling voices conveying a bad scene. I was at the rear of a 12-man column on a recon patrol looking for a suspected Viet Cong bunker complex fifty miles south of Saigon. Earlier that day my six man team had linked up with Sgt. Newman's team because there was danger that we could run into a VC concentration—at least that's what intelligence reported.

Newman is hit," cracked my radio. "Grenade booby trap. He's bleeding bad."

"Call Medavac. Be careful about others. I'm coming up."

I wasn't feeling at all calm or confident. We were on the edge of a partially overgrown abandoned rice paddy abutting a thickly wooded area of unknown size that we were planning to probe for Viet Cong presence. We had been moving toward the woods in search of evidence and now we had it in the most unwelcome of circumstances. Booby traps were often clustered on the perimeter of VC controlled territory. Now we had a casualty, the explosion and yelling exposed our presence and location, and the mission leadership had passed to me. We had to secure the area for the Medavac helicopter, avoid additional casualties, establish a defendable position to counter a VC response while getting Newman out alive.

Newman had been leading and walking point for the combined team patrol. In addition to his often demonstrated courage and combat sense, over the past eight months he had become a very good friend. Others in Company E had been killed or wounded during my tour, but none were close friends. In fact Newman already had two purple hearts acquired after receiving accidental shrapnel wounds from our own explosives. We often joked he needed to actually earn one before leaving country. Today the black humor didn't seem very funny as I tried to concentrate on each step while moving quickly forward.

Newman couldn't quite believe his situation. He was conscious, not panicked, but shaken. In a semi-sitting position on the ground, except for a pale expression, Newman looked normal. The wounds were all on his backside. He had tripped the device and walked a step or two beyond before it exploded.

"Saw the three sticks," he said, "but not the device."

Three sticks or three rocks grouped together were one symbol used by the VC to mark "danger" zones and warn civilians away.

We set up a defensive perimeter and waited. We took no return fire. The woods were silent. Medavac, accompanied by gunships, arrived within 15 minutes of the call.

"He's lost a lot of blood," the medic yelled over the noise of the Huey's engine as they hoisted Newman on the litter. "He took it in a lot of places and we've got to move him quickly."

Only then did I understand how bad his condition was. The Medavac lifted off leaving open the question if I would see him again. I said a prayer and moved the team out. We wanted to shoot some gooks.

Title: Body Count
Setting: Shade
Location: Vietnam Delta
Date: September 1969

We were in a Huey on a parakeet mission accompanied by a Cobra gunship. Five of us set with legs hanging out of the doorless Huey searching areas of suspected Viet Cong activity. The day was clear, good flying and visual observation weather. We were flying tree top level across declared free fire zones that were "pacified" because no one, by South Vietnam government law, was authorized to be in the area.

"Two running in the open," radioed the Cobra pilot as the miniguns opened fire. "I think I got one."

"We'll go in and take a look," I responded as the Huey drove downward on the Cobra's marking round.

Off the chopper, we were in waist deep grass and brush. We moved cautiously with the Cobra and the Huey giving close overhead cover. After several minutes we saw one body, without question Viet Cong.

"One KIA," I radioed.

"Roger that. I'm sure there were two and he couldn't have run far," responded the Cobra pilot.

We continued the search. Within the large field were several clumps of taller brush. "We'll check those brush clumps," I said and split the team into two with one helicopter giving supporting cover to each team.

Our M-16's were locked, loaded, on full automatic with safety's off. Where was the other? Was he armed? Were these scouts for a larger party? Had we stumbled into a deployment maneuver?

Crouched and anxious we approached one of the clumps of brush. Slowly. Step. Wait. Listen. Look. Step. Silence. Then the sense of unseen movement 6 feet ahead. Instincts, training, fear and weapon simultaneously reacted. The young man went down without a sound. He took three or four rounds in the chest. Silence.

"Another KIA," I reported. "Keep searching."

Thirty minutes later we departed with several Viet Cong documents and photographs that were turned over to intelligence. The younger man may have been in his late teens and did not have a weapon that we could find. I've always wondered if he was trying to stand up to surrender. Maybe he didn't know what to say or was too frightened for words.

Title: Urn
Setting: Hazy sun
Location: South of My Tho
Date: October 1969

Across Vietnam's Delta ceramic clay urns holding twenty to fifty gallons of water clustered nearby the thatched huts. The virtually indestructible urns would last for decades, even generations unless blown to bits by a C-4 charge, a grenade or M-60 machine gun target practice. The water in the urns served the needs of the residents and occasionally American soldiers, particularly during the dry season. Carrying water was an added weight for the Rangers who preferred to travel as light as possible. If a few more rounds of ammo could be substituted for an extra canteen, some found this an acceptable tradeoff. The problem of the urn water was not so much the microscopic bugs that couldn't be seen and could cause illness. The iodine pills were stronger than the bacteria. More difficult were the visible bugs, gnats, mosquitoes and miscellaneous insects that floated, swam or lay on the surface forming a thin translucent scum over the water. A vertical look down on the earth tone urns captured the otherwise unseen aquatic life at play in the rural villager's precious fresh water source.

Title: Futility
Setting: Starlight
Location: Mekong River
Date: November 1969

Insertion of Rangers into mission areas represented one of the most dangerous parts of an operation. The helicopters were fast, convenient, under gunship cover, but noisy and hardly clandestine. In the Delta, the abundance of waterways, canals and rivers provided an option for boat insertion because the Navy operated a variety of craft that could move in low light or bad weather conditions as well as maintaining an agreeable level of quietness. The boats also offered the bonus of a Navy prepared dinner prior to the mission that was by tradition and definition far superior to whatever the Army could provide.

In the fall of 1969 our six-man team sat low in the bow of a small Navy craft without power as it rode the river current down stream toward a preselected insertion point. Darkness had fallen but enough moon shone that the river's shore features could be used as guide points. The captain nosed the craft into a cove and the team slid into waist deep water moving as quickly as possible up the slick muddy bank. Pushing several meters through thick river side brush, we came to the edge of a large open area of rice paddies. We spread out to form a defensive and observation alignment, tucking in behind the paddy dikes to watch and listen.

The area had been "cleared" by an ARVN-9th Division combined infantry sweep the day before. The combined forces had encountered no contact with the VC; intelligence reported that the VC had mostly moved out of the area representing a success for the "pacification" program. We had been sent back to determine if the VC were using the area as a night transit route and to set up an ambush for any enemy that showed up.

Some 100 meters from our location, half a dozen hooches were clustered. These small hamlets were common throughout the Delta and populated by the women, old men, and children. Male adults were either hiding out with the VC or in the South Vietnamese Army. The U.S. Government policy of turning the war over to the South Vietnamese was showcased in the Delta with the partial pull out of the 9th Division in the summer of 1969. The VC threat in the Delta had been officially contained.

With this backdrop we scanned the area with a Starlight scope on an evening that made the technology perform splendidly. The greenish outlines of the hooches were crisp and the breadth of the viewing field gave us confidence in the security of our position. We were alert but relaxed.

About midnight one of the Rangers whispered, "Look at this."

Taking the scope, I watched a column of men nonchalantly emerge from a far wood-line and walk, single file along a paddy dike trail toward the hamlet. Some carried weapons but none seemed wary or on alert. As they approached the hamlet, they were greeted as if the visit was expected and apparent social pleasantries were exchanged. Clearly we were witnessing the nocturnal infrastructure of the Viet Cong and the political-social fabric of the North Vietnamese-Viet Cong war effort that our side had not been able to destroy. Within the hour our surprise assault disrupted this particular rendezvous, but the image of VC moving with impunity and lack of fear in areas reported to be secure for the South Vietnamese government suggested that the war's balance had tilted away from the South Vietnam and its "foreign" ally.

Title: Servant Girl
Setting: Bright sun
Location: Tan An Fire Base
Date: December 1969

An attractive young girl, 16 years old, named Tan worked for the Ranger Company at Tan An. (The Rangers commented among themselves that all 18 year old Vietnamese women were beautiful, but the harshness of the war made them old and wrinkled by twenty-five.) Tan had been around long enough doing laundry, mending and related chores so that she picked up a little English. Mostly she worked for the officers and senior enlisted types so I didn't have a lot of interaction with her. One day, however, she was doing some seamstress work outside and we talked a bit. Her family was local and she had gone to school for a few years so she could read and write. But when the Americans offered some needed income she came to work on the base. I asked if she had been to Saigon about 50 kilometers north.

"No, but I have heard about it."
"Where is Saigon?" I asked.
"Somewhere far from here."
"And where is America?" I continued.
"It's a long way from here, too," Tan replied.

Smart Charlie

By Jack Bick

When bullets are whizzing past your head, it doesn't matter how big the war is or how long you are going to be in it. However, in the great scope of history, the Vietnam War was fairly easy. Unlike WWII, the soldier knew when he would go home. It didn't matter how hard each individual soldier fought because the leaders were not fighting to win. That is what made the Vietnam War so hard to take. There was no "sense of purpose" or hope of achieving a victory. The goal was to survive for 365 days.

Let's get back to the bullets whizzing past my head. If one of those bullets hits its mark, life is over on this earth; nothing left to reflect on. However, the near death experience is a seed for continuous cultivation of thought.

Questions arise such as "Why was I spared?", "How close to death was I?", "What did I do right that saved my life?" or "Does God have something for me to do?"

My personal philosophy is that everything fits into God's plan. What he wants me to do is not necessarily dramatic or newsworthy like curing cancer. Maybe it was just to come home and try to be a good husband, father, friend, newspaper publisher and worshiper.

Here are some personal brushes with death that inspire me to try to be a good person because God allowed me to continue to experience this wonderful life.

There was constant reminder that war was at hand and that the enemy could strike at any time. The road into Dong Tam, the command base for the 9th Division, was not a straight line. The road made a 90-degree turn toward the gate and then there was an abrupt c-shaped curve before reaching the guardhouse. That would prevent any vehicle from speeding into the gate.

Barbed wire was everywhere. One foot diameter coils on fences, five-foot coils around building and perimeters. Concrete bunkers as well as sand bag reinforced wood bunkers were not only on the perimeter, but also throughout the camp in case of a mortar attack.

Even our sand volleyball court was strategically located next to a bunker, which was further encapsulated by putting an NCO club on top.

In the base camp you could also smell and hear the war. The smell of fuel was ever present and the sound of helicopters pierced the air with the stuttered sound of the blades cutting the air and the change in pitch as the pilot maneuvered the machine.

The most significant sounds of war are gunshots and explosions. My first experience was poignant because of the circumstance not the closeness of the fire. In the Mekong Delta there is water and mud everywhere. Even though it had not rained for some time, our boots were covered in mud. Despite the mud encrusted boots, I had to cross a 10-foot log over a small stream. There was very little water in the stream a few feet below the log. The best way to cross is to look six feet ahead of your feet and step quickly.

Gunfire broke the silence as I placed my second step on the log. I pushed off hard and jumped to the bank of the stream. Bullets were making a "thump" sound as they entered the mud on the other side of the stream.

The other soldiers fell back from the stream, found cover and returned fire. Those who had already crossed were hugging the ground and crawling for cover. By this time the VC were either dead or running out of the area. I don't remember if we got a body count but we were all OK except for my camera, which was ruined in the mud and water.

On another operation we were receiving small arms fire on a sporadic basis from many different angles. The lieutenant could not determine whether there were one or two enemies shooting and moving to simulate a large number of troops, or if there was indeed a large force in front of us.

He decided to bring in artillery and radioed the coordinates to fire command. It was the first time that I heard incoming artillery hissing, then thundering toward its target. My thought was one of relief that it was not headed to my location. The intended strike zone was about 500 meters in front of us but the shell landed about 100 meters away. Luckily we had all instinctively hunkered down as the shell passed over us because shrapnel rained all around us.

Frantically, the lieutenant redirected the next shell for a greater distance. Normally, the procedure would be to drop the shell at the longest distance to hit the enemy and then walk the shells toward your location. On that day the tactic was reversed.

One of the scariest situations did not involve any firing of bullets or artillery. I was flying a "parakeet mission" with the Ranger unit at dawn; that is, hopping around on a helicopter accompanied by two gunships and dropping in at selected sites with complete surprise. The air was still hazy and we were flying fast and low looking for any signs of life in an area that had been defoliated, probably with Agent Orange. Anyone found in a defoliated area was considered to be the enemy—man, woman or child.

The entire area was void of color. The trees were still there but with no leaves and the trunks had a deathly gray look. The grasses and weeds were tan, dry and lifeless. Even the bare earth had a pale look, a dead look. The entire atmosphere that morning was of dread and despair.

The chopper took a quick turn and landed so we could check out a hooch that could be a hiding place for the enemy. There was evidence that someone was using the hooch, but no one was in it now; not even in the earthen bunker inside the hooch. The enemy was probably still near, so it was decided to call in the chopper allowing us to look from the air. As the chopper approached we lined up three men on each side. Boarding the craft, a vulnerable time, must only take a second or two.

Everyone boarded. I had grabbed the leg of the seat to pull myself in, but it gave way and I was still on the ground as the chopper started to ascend. The rest of the sequence only took 15-20 seconds, but in my memory it plays in slow motion. The standard operating procedure is to have the helicopter make a one-minute circle and then come in for a pickup. Recently I had documented a similar circumstance, so instinctively I dropped to the ground in the high grass, hoping that the VC had not seen me miss the pickup.

The men on the chopper informed the pilot of the situation and he responded by hovering. This put the tail rotor right above my head. What a way to give my life for my country—a slab of meat chopped by a blender.

The Rangers told the pilot to go around as the SOP commands. Realizing the danger I was in, he moved the chopper 20 feet away coming to a full landing. The Rangers, realizing that the pilot isn't going to follow procedure, yelled to me to crawl to the chopper and board. Luckily, we received no fire.

The Ranger team leader radioed the incident to his command. We were met at the heliport by the Ranger Commanding Officer and the pilot's superior, who grounded him for not following the right course of action and endangering the lives of ten men.

Helicopters were an everyday part of life. I made 48 combat assaults, which wasn't a large number for a combat soldier, but it was significant for a correspondent. As a correspondent I had a considerable amount of freedom to choose my missions and where I would go. One particular day there was good intelligence that a large unit of VC was operating in and area close to the Mekong River, yet away from any villages. The plan was to put troops in along the river and move the enemy away from the river. Once they started moving, our unit would be inserted by air to surround them.

This was an area that I had seen from the air many times flying with the lieutenant colonel. It was heavily wooded, very few hooches, lots of small streams, canals and ditches for irrigation. This area provided an abundance of cover for the enemy and very few landing zones for helicopters.

There were six helicopters, which needed to make two sorties to get all the troops to the field. The officer in charge of the unit, a captain, asked me to accompany him and the radioman on the second sortie. I did not have to comply and I really wanted to go in with the first group to get photos of a hot landing or hot LZ. I consented on the condition that if we made a second insertion that day, I would go in with the first troops. I had a feeling we were going to be hopping around looking for the concentration of the enemy. Both initial sorties were uneventful. We spent the morning combing through the heavy vegetation and trees and all we encountered were insects that stuck to our sweating bodies. The sun was high in the sky, the heat was oppressive and the enemy was smart enough to dig in and not move around like we were doing.

The lieutenant colonel was getting frustrated. He knew there was a large force of the enemy within our large perimeter and we could not find, engage and kill them. We were ordered back to our original LZ because there were so few available and the others were a long distance away. The lieutenant colonel didn't want to use up his troops walking, he wanted them fresh for another assault.

One of the cardinal rules in the field is not to use the same zone, especially on the same day. There is a risk that Charlie would booby-trap the area. Most booby-traps were land mines that had to be triggered by trip wires that were almost impossible to detect.

The birds flew in a formation of two rows, three on each side. We were instructed to line up where we disembarked and be on the lookout for booby traps and trip wires. The atmosphere was charged because we knew the folly of using the same zone and because we were sure to have a hot LZ at the other end of the ride.

The captain and I lined up together. He nodded my way and instructed a private to change places with me for the next ride.

Since I was out with a full line company, I only carried a sidearm, no rifle.

As we waited for the choppers the men were checking their rifles and adjusting grenades and clips, so they could reload and react to what the enemy had to throw at them. I checked my cameras and preset the focus because there is no time to think about that with lead in the air.

The destination did not seem far away but the choppers were going to loop around in order to add more surprise to our arrival. We lifted off and everyone exchanged glances of relief that no booby traps exploded. Our minds quickly refocused on the landing, our faces turned serious. No one looked anyone else in the eye so as not to detect any fear.

The birds dropped to the treetops and suddenly made a hard turn and landed in a small open area. Just as quick, they were gone to get the second contingent of our company. We dropped to the ground checking every leaf and twig in the wood-lines that surrounded us. No response from the enemy. Someone yelled to spread out and secure the zone but stay out of the wood-line. That's when we heard the explosion, then another.

The chopper I had been on, the one that I would have been waiting for, hit a trip wire and two booby traps exploded. Of the ten men, four on the crew and six combat soldiers, all were killed or required amputation to save their lives. God had spared me.

That incident proved to me that Charlie was smart and that underestimating him would be a dangerous choice.

Most of the time I had to think as a journalist. My mind dwelt on what to write about, where the best story would be, what could be a good photo—that was what I was trained to do all those years in college. Yet that one week of combat training at Ft. Riley Kansas was the education that kept me alive in Vietnam. This next incident earned me the Army Commendation Medal for Valor. I was not heroic, I was merely trying to survive and in the process, helped a few others to survive. The captain who wrote me up for the award said that it would be the illustration to the world that I was in the field with combat soldiers. They were awarded the Combat Infantryman's Badge (CIB) and this valor award would be my CIB.

The day began rather uneventfully as the infantry company moved from wood-line to wood-line interrupted by small openings of tall grass. My recollection of the event is almost like an out of body experience, it occurred so fast and I was numb afterwards. It took me a few hours to feel normal again.

Part of our unit went sweeping through a wooded area ahead of us. The remainder of the unit was sweeping through the wooded area behind and there were five of us in the open—the captain, radioman, a machine gunner, a rifleman and myself.

Nine times out of ten Charlie would open fire high, then gain control of the AK-47, then bring the fire down to the target. During this encounter, we were hugging the ground by the time Charlie got control. There was more than one firing at us, but there was no telling how many were in that wood-line. The captain immediately radioed to get help, but we needed to return fire immediately or die. Carrying only a 38-caliber pistol, I crawled over to the machine gunner. I returned fire while he fed the weapon. We had gained fire superiority by the time our troops came to the clearing, because Charlie had stopped firing and started running.

Over the years, throughout business and throughout my personal life, there have been tests of my nerves, of my willingness to act or my ability to succeed, however none put my life in jeopardy. I can look back on these experiences and know that God not only gave me the opportunity to be here now, but he gave me an inner strength to overcome challenges.

It is my desire to revisit Vietnam. I understand that the people are warm and open to Americans and that the country is moving slowly toward a market economy and a better life for its people. We may have lost the war but we also may have achieved some good anyway.

When I do visit, I'm going down Highway 1 south of Saigon (Ho Chi Minh City) to see if a certain sign is still there:

TAN AN CITY
THE PEACEFUL CITY
KEEP IT THAT WAY
U S DRIVERS

A More Than Typical Non-Mission Day

aka: The Shitter

by Paul A. Newman

Staff Sergeant Turner developed what he called a "case of the ass". There is no dictionary definition sufficient to explain the term; instead, one must look to a series of occurrences and frustrations from the lower level soldier's point of view in attempting to rationalize the senior soldier's irrational orders. Little niggling looks, statements, or orders continue to build resentment, frustration, anger, hatred, and/or contempt. This is a story of how one soldier dealt with his "case of the ass" in one day.

Morning formation, held before six o'clock was routine.

"Ten hut!" Hollered Sergeant First Class Brooking. "Report!" He directed his showy tone to the squad leaders at the end of each row.

Each squad claimed to be "all present and accounted for, Sergeant." Brooking knew better. He hadn't been in this man's army for twenty-eight years for nothing. He knew when these kids were trying to pull something. And these kids, Rangers at that, always tried to pull something.

Sergeant First Class Brooking, a veteran of Korea and the big one, WWII, had been assigned to the Ranger unit at Dong Tam, Co E, 75th Inf, Rangers only two months before it was transferred to Tan An as part of President Nixon's attempt to give the country back to the Vietnamese. The attempt was working, as the troops pulled back, the Vietnamese, the VC, not the South Vietnamese, moved in. They were getting their country back. Sergeant Brooking, (we can drop the word "first" for the reason that it only signifies three stripes on top and two rockers on the bottom) was taking over for the actual First Sergeant (differentiated by three stipes on top and three rockers on the bottom) who was in the hospital with a wound inflicted as a consequence of a mortar attack that got lucky. Brooking, (we can drop the word "sergeant" to show our contempt of his status as part of the "case of the ass") was in his glory. It was obvious that he would never be a First Sergeant, but he reveled in the position of First Sergeant. He played it to the hilt, much to the disdain of the troops who only had contempt for him because he refused to go out on a single mission with the active Rangers. He wore the beret with pride, but the Rangers knew that he didn't earn it—at least to their knowledge, he didn't earn it in this war at Dong Tam or Tan An. In fact, other than the knowledge that he had been in the Korean conflict, the troops had no idea what he had done in that war. Nor, sadly was the case, did they care.

Brooking was not liked. He refused missions. From a practical point of view, now that I am the age Brooking was, there was nothing wrong with his perspective. One can get killed on missions outside Tan An. However, from the position of a twenty year old Ranger, who did go on missions and risked his life and health, if the man didn't go on missions then he shouldn't wear the beret. He was a fraud. And, he was chicken shit. And, he drank too much and his face was puffy from it along with his midline that he attempted to pull in to look sharp, but which didn't work. Well, it is admitted that most of the troops drank too much, but after all they were fighting the actual war. But to drink and not fight the war was—why, it was incongruous to these twenty year olds.

"Toth, where is Turner?" Sternly demanded Brooking.

"Ummm, I guess he is still in bed, Sergeant," he answered hearing suppressed giggles.

"You, a team leader, didn't report him absent, did you, Toth?"

"Why no, Sergeant." Oh boy, here it comes, thought Toth, more bullshit.

"Hmmm,...Sergeant Toth, your team will do detail on the shit barrels. Right after breakfast, Toth, your team will get rid of the shit barrels in the four seater—the one behind the NCO barracks. You got that, Sergeant Toth?"

Oh he was so precise. He so enjoyed giving this shit detail to Toth. Toth, known for his wild man tactics in the field, was so liked by the men. This will knock him down a peg or two.

"I got that, Sergeant First Class Brooking," he shouted with the force of an Airborne Ranger response. More giggles.

"And you, Rhodes, your team and Turner's team will take the shitter apart, board by board and dispose of it in a proper manner. Do you think you can accomplish that mission, Sergeant Rhodes?" asked Brooking in a superior, supercilious and snotty manner.

"Yes, Sergeant," he answered. No lip there.

"Good, the rest of you will report to me after breakfast. Now let's police the area. Line up. If you have a mission tonight, you don't have to report to me, but there is only one team going out, so I have some nice juicy details for you." The troops groaned and mumbled lining up for police call.

Brooking hollered, "Rhodes, tell Turner I want to see him right after breakfast."

"Yes, Sergeant."

Even when the Top Sergeant wasn't injured and sitting in the hospital, Brooking was in charge of details. Under the standard operating procedure, he assigned details after the morning formation, and then disappeared for the remainder of the day. When a team leader looked for him to report on the status of the detail, he was nowhere to be found. That suited the troops well. Over time, when the first detail was completed, the troops considered the rest of the day as their own time.

Brooking had an uncommunicative air about him. His orders to the troops rarely elicited a response unless it was a muttered response under their breath, cursing him or his supposed cowardice for failing to go out on a mission. The usual comments heard were: "fucking lifer, fucking bastard, fucking commie, fucking chicken." They were not complimentary; but, given the gentlemen courtesy of the Rangers, they were not said to his face.

There was a lapse in leadership and a lapse in communication. If Brooking had gone out on a mission or two it would have showed the boys he was one of them; not a coward, a Ranger. But he didn't go out on missions. The Top Sergeant went out infrequently, but he went out. That created a bond. If Brooking would have at least told some of the troops that he was at Bastogne or Inchon, it might have made a difference. But no one knew what he had done in his two previous wars. Hence, there was no justification in their minds that he was anything other than a chicken-shit E-7. And Rangers didn't like chicken-shit E-7's telling them what to do. Their resentment congealed.

Brooking drank daily. Since he was acting First Sergeant, his mornings seemed clearer, but his evenings were spent in his room or at the NCO club nursing a scotch, neat. By six every evening, he was in torpor. No one knew what drove him to this state, or if he just inched into it like addictive alcoholics do. In looking at the Rangers, they were a hard drinking crowd. A number of them would be in Brooking's shoes at Brooking's age, but they couldn't see that. They were just looking to survive the next mission, to go home, to arrive at DEROS date. They looked forward, Brooking looked back.

* * * *

Sergeant Toth entered Staff Sergeant Turner's room and slammed the door. Turner, awakened, eyed him sleepily.

"Who the fuck does he think he is? I always get assigned these shit details." Angry, he plopped onto Turner's chair and put his feet on the footlocker.

"What time is it?"

"Eight-thirty. You missed breakfast. Brooking wants to see you. He looked for you at formation. You got shit detail too."

"What shit?"

"You and Rhodes have to tear down the shitter."

"What shitter?"

"The one out back."

"Our shitter? What for? Where do we shit?"

"Shit, how the shit do I know. We can shit our pants for all he cares, fuckin lifer," he paused, "but you better be getting up. He's going to come here if you don't go there."

"Yeah, yeah."

Toth was not a favorite of Brooking's. Toth was a favorite of Turner's. On a hunter-killer mission Toth loved to be the hunter team. He loved to kill people—legally. He was thin, wiry, Italian. He talked too loud, too obnoxiously. He bitched constantly, complained too loudly. Everyone heard him and it caused him to be only a Sergeant, instead of a Staff Sergeant. But he was good in the field. He wanted to shoot gooks. He had thirty-two notches on his rifle stock. How he could scratch the fiberglass/plastic—who knows; but he did. And, he considered himself very Christian, he didn't count women or children.

Toth was rich. He had collected seven Chinese AK-47's, three nine millimeter pistols, and many photos and trinkets. He sent an AK home; foil-wrapped in individual pieces here and there stuffed into speakers, a refrigerator and presents. He got the entire rifle home.

Brooking didn't like the voice timbre of Toth. It grated on him. It grated on everyone, but if you saw him in the field, you overlooked it. Brooking never saw him in the field, so it grated all the more. That voice got Toth all the shit details.

"Where's Rhodes?" asked Turner.

"Talking to Brooking in the orderly room."

Turner dressed slowly, picking up speed as he wakened.

"You realize we are going to have to walk a mile to take a shit if we get rid of that shitter?"

"No shit, Dick Tracy. Why do you think we all have a 'case of the ass'," he paused, "and I get to clean up the shit, again." Toth punched his fist. "I ought to dump them in his room."

Turner laughed.

* * * *

Rhodes was sitting on the bench in the Orderly Room as Turner entered.

"Why didn't you wake me up?"

"I did," answered Rhodes.

"Oh," whispered Turner.

Brooking entered from the Captain's office, looked at Rhodes and Turner and shook his head sadly. "Where were you for formation?"

"Guess I overslept, Sarge."

"Yeah, again." Brooking hesitated a moment trying to decide if he should lambast Turner for missing formation or forget it. Another confrontation. These young kids. No discipline. He decided to forgo the argument. "You have no mission today? Either of you, right?"

"Right."

Brooking, attempting to hide his grin, said, "You get to destroy the shitter behind the NCO barracks. When you're done, report back to me." Brooking beamed. He hadn't been so delighted since he had his last scotch. He loved to give these ugly little details to the troops causing him his little leadership problems…a lesson learned young fellow.

"Hey, Sarge. I have a question. Why are we tearing it down, it's almost brand new? If we tear it down, we're going to have to walk all the way over to artillery to take a shit."

"That's really too bad, isn't it. You will have to walk somewhere," he smiled, then said, "It is too close to the barracks, it's unsanitary. That is Army regulations, soldier." His tone indicated no response was necessary.

"What about the officer shitter?"

"That stays."

"Army regulations, right Sarge?"

"Whatever works, soldier. Get to it." Brooking was getting angry at the flippancy of this Staff Sergeant. His face turned red. "I don't want to see a trace of that shitter when you are done. Do you understand your mission, soldier?"

"Yes, Sergeant," Turner answered nasally.

* * * *

Turner was still laughing as he and Rhodes approached the shitter. The two teams were sitting against the barracks wall. Assorted tools, picks, sledge hammers, and crow bars were lying in the sand. They knew their mission and they talked about the best method to accomplish it. "Burn it." "Too close to the barracks." "Paint it the color of sand, Brooking won't see it." "He might bump into it." "Move it." "What?" "Move it." "Now that's not a bad idea." "No, that's a good idea." "Where the fuck do we move it?" "How the fuck do we move it?" "Sell it." "Gooks?" "Would they buy it?" "Why not, lot's of good wood there!" "What about the shit?" "Where's Toth's team, they're supposed to do the shit." "You won't see them today." "Leave it, the gooks can use it for something." "They'll probably sell it back to us."

The strategy was decided, the logistics were discussed, the mission plan plotted, the equipment identified, the duties of each member and team leader defined and the mission was on. The troops were elated. Break time before the hard work began. Be back on site at ten hundred hours ready to go.

* * * *

Turner went back to the barracks with Rhodes. Toth was laying on Rhodes's bunk.

"Aren't you going to do the shit?" Asked Turner.

"Fuck that shit! He gives me the shit detail every time. I ain't doin it."

"I think we might solve your problem, but you've got to help us. We're going to move the shitter and sell it to the gooks."

Toth sat up, grinned. "Good idea. Solves my problem."

"I'm going to get the truck. You get the guys refreshments. It's already too hot out there. Everyone is sweating and we haven't done anything yet."

Turner went to sign out the deuce and a half truck. As he approached the Orderly Room, Brooking came out of the office, looked at Turner and demanded: "Why aren't your men tearing down the shitter?"

"We're right on it Sarge."

"No, Sergeant Turner, I asked you 'Why aren't your men tearing down the shitter?', I did not ask you if you were on it. Now why?" Maclean glared at Turner.

"Sarge, we'll have it done by noon. If we do, do we get the rest of the day off?" Turner smiled, placating, half-hearted appealing.

"It's already ten, Sergeant Turner." He glared, turned abruptly and left. How do you argue with a smiling, flippant youngster?

* * * *

Turner backed the two and a half ton truck within three feet of the shitter. Rhodes roped the undercarriage. Three separate ropes were tied to the shitter. The shitter was erected on three slats of two by tens to keep it off the ground. It was a four seater. Under each seat was a one-third portion of a fifty gallon drum designed to collect the troopers rejections; and, probably, ejections. Generally, a detail was formed to remove the drums, add kerosene, light and stir it until the mess disappeared. The drums were approximately one third full of shit, pee and toilet paper. Inside the shitter, the odor was—shit.

The three teams stood around drinking beer obtained by Toth while Rhodes coordinated the tie on. The shitter was firmly attached by ropes. It was ready to drag. Time for another break. These details have to be spaced correctly.

"Okay," said Turner, "time for a break. I can see Rhodes sweating his buns off. Meet back here in fifteen minutes. We don't need everyone, let's see, me, Rhodes, Toth, Booth and Konavalov, and Tex—Tex, you can sell it, right?—should be able to get it done. The rest of you can take time off. Keep out of Brooking's way and there should be no problem."

"It's already eleven hundred, he's stoned by now," Toth said.

* * * *

Rhodes, Toth and Turner went into the NCO barracks. Toth pulled out a pipe, filled it with material that looked like tobacco from a small plastic bag, and lit it. He passed it to Turner. Rhodes sipped a coke.

"Fuck, it's hot!" said Toth.

"Yeah, no shit. Hey you missed Brooking trying to chew me out when I went to sign out the truck. He's pissed we aren't getting the job done the way he wants it," said Turner.

"The guy has a problem. A personality problem, in addition to his alcohol problem," added Rhodes.

"Man, I'd sure like to get that mother out in the field," said Toth.

"That's why he doesn't go." Rhodes responded.

"One burst in the back of the head," said Toth, reeling as if he was shooting a burst from his M-16. "That's all it would take."

"Then he'd get a purple heart, posthumously," Rhodes said. "Do you really think you could just shoot one of your own men?"

"Sure! I could frag him too!"

Rhodes was agitated. "Toth, that is crazy. You might hate his guts, but you don't shoot one of your own."

They sat there. Toth inhaling deep, holding it, and blowing it out. He passed it to Turner.

"You know what would be neat?" asked Turner.

"Yeah, blow the fucker up."

"Nah, but how about…blow him up mentally. Blow him up just a little bit. Shake him up."

"You mean a blanket party?"

"No, I mean really shake him up. What would he do if he found a grenade under his pillow. Not a live one, a dud."

Rhodes sat up, looked interested.

"We can break off the blasting cap, blow the fuse, and re-cock it. When he hears it pop, he will literally shit his pants. No harm, no foul."

Toth grinned, inhaled. Smiled, as he held his breath. Rhodes got on his knees and dragged a box of grenades from under the bunk.

"Don't touch it, we have to make sure there are no fingerprints. CID has a way to chase these things down. We might want to put the box back in supplies when we are done so they can't chase the box down, too," said Turner.

"We are in this together, gentlemen," said Rhodes, "no one says a thing. No bragging Toth. You understand?"

Toth nodded affirmatively, still holding his breath, grinning.

Rhodes put his hand in a tee shirt, took out a grenade, handed the shirt and grenade to Turner. Turner unscrewed the cap and broke off the blasting cap. He pulled the ring and dropped the head on the floor. They all backed up. Toth let his breath out with a whoosh. Four seconds, it popped and fizzed. The fuse was blown. Turner picked it up, re-cocked the spring, put the pin in, screwed the head back on, and handed it to Toth. No one had spoken during the process. They looked at one another.

"Under the pillow, Toth."

"I hope the pillow is heavy enough to hold the spring."

"I watch the front, Rhodes, you watch the back. In two minutes we meet back at the truck. And, we got to keep quiet. Got it Toth."

"Not a word, not to anyone."

* * * *

Rhodes signaled Toth, thumbs up. Turner signaled, thumbs up. Toth walked the platform walk to Brooking's room, quietly entered. He was inside for less than thirty seconds and walked hurriedly to the deuce and a half. Rhodes went the long way around. Turner backtracked.

Toth chugged a beer. Turner felt the pipe effect. Turner took a beer and climbed into the truck. Tex got into the passenger seat, the rest of the team got into the back, except for Rhodes who checked the drag on the shitter to make sure it was going to work. Turner edged the truck forward, the ropes tightened, the shitter moved forward.

"Works!" Shouted Rhodes.

Toth jumped from the truck, ran into the barracks and came out with a pistol, his M-16 and a bandolier of clips. "Just in case."

The shitter was wider than the truck by eighteen inches on each side. The route taken was around the mess hall to the main road, then a right turn to the main gate. Rhodes climbed in back.

The truck moved forward. It was better to keep the truck moving than to start and stop—to maintain momentum. As the truck turned the corner by the mess hall, the edge of the shitter collided with the one thousand gallon water trailer. The water buffalo was pulled over on its side. Turner kept moving. Booth and Tex yelled at Turner, that he knocked over the water buffalo. Turner looked in the side mirror, saw the cook run out the door from the mess hall and raise his fist, shouting at them. Turner kept moving.

The shitter turned the corner to the main drag easily. The MP's at the main gate called the truck to a halt. Checking in the shitter, they laughed and waved the truck on.

The streets were packed with vendors, motorcycles, bicyclists, walkers. Natives stared at the truck pulling the shitter with a bunch of black berets standing in the truck bed. Little kids pointed their fingers and ran alongside the truck. Toth kept yelling at the kids to "Di di mau".

The shitter sideswiped a bus. The bus stopped and the driver got out to inspect the damage. Turner kept the truck moving. He wasn't stopping for anything.

The white helmeted traffic cop smiled at them, stopped all traffic and let the truck pass.

The kids running alongside clamored for candy. "GI, number one, candy?"

Toth yelled obscenities, "Fucking gooks, number ten."

Tex directed Turner where to stop. He dismounted and went looking for a buyer. After five minutes, he came back and said he found a buyer for forty dollars worth of piasters only. No military payment currency. That was ok. Tex climbed in and directed Turner around the block and to swerve it so that the shitter was in front of the buyers home. Tex exchanged the money with the two women buyers. Rhodes, Booth and Konovalov unhooked the shitter. They all climbed aboard.

No one had entered the shitter, yet. As they pulled away, one of the women came out of the shitter yelling. By her actions it was clear she discovered the shit barrels for which she just paid forty dollars. Turner didn't stop. They all laughed.

As they drove into the compound, they saw the water buffalo had been righted. That was quick. Turner signed the truck back in at 1145. He checked into the orderly room to report the detail was finished, then told the clerk. Brooking wasn't there. Must be the rest of the day off.

* * * *

At formation the following morning, nothing was said about the water buffalo. Nothing was said about the shitter detail. Brooking did not appear. Sergeant Jones handled formation. The Captain made an appearance and announced that the team leaders would stay after formation. The Captain looked at each of the team leaders and announced that Sergeant Brooking would not be back for several days. However, a grenade was found in Sergeant Brooking's room. Your Captain is greatly distressed. CID has been called in. It is up to you team leaders to find out who put the grenade in Sergeant Brooking's room. There is a one hundred dollar reward for information leading to the arrest of the person who put the grenade in the room. No, he wouldn't give any of the particulars. Yes, there may be a greater reward.

"Does anyone have any information?"

No one spoke.

The Captain spoke: "I can tell you, your Captain now has a thorough 'case of the ass!' Dismissed."

Nine Lessons From The Ninth

by Bob Wallace

When asked what happened while in Vietnam, I fumble to respond. Being neither a good storyteller nor a particularly keen observer of detail and nuance, efforts to tell about war often result in the questioner losing interest long before my tales are finished. Therefore, with brevity as a guide, these nine lessons for life, drawn from twelve months in Vietnam's Delta with the 75th Rangers of the Ninth Infantry Division, capture the essence of whatever story I might tell. (Those who suggested development of Seventy-five Life Lessons from the 75th Infantry Rangers will remain disappointed.)

Lesson one: Not everyone wears a watch.
Lesson two: Separated combatants produce better cease-fires.
Lesson three: Chopsticks work well for their intended purpose.
Lesson four: Imposition may be opportunity.
Lesson five: The Psalms are contemporary literature.
Lesson six: Killing communists is easier if you don't see them.
Lesson seven: Intelligence requires field verification.
Lesson eight: Trust the front line.

Lesson nine: Tough times make us laugh.

Not everyone wears a watch

The company commander gave me a Seiko wristwatch when I left Vietnam in January, 1970. The ceremony, if there was one, is forgotten. The Seiko had become the traditional gift from Company E, 75th Rangers to departing soldiers. As memorabilia, it might have some meaning today except I recall giving it away soon after getting back to the States to a friend who actually wore it. I always had a pretty good sense of time so considered a wrist watch another unnecessary thing to either break or lose.

I was just glad to get out of Vietnam alive and uninjured. I rejected the option to remain there another 90 days in exchange for an early out from the Army. There were absolutely no regrets until early February when the news reported that American forces "invaded" Cambodia. I speculated that Company E might have gone in a few days before the announcement. They had. For a brief moment I wished I had been with them. They were doing what should have been done long before. The North Vietnam Army (NVA) and Viet Cong (VC) were in and out of Cambodia like old men in a bar going to the restroom. Cambodia had been R&R territory for them. So I was proud to hear Company E got in there early. I didn't need the watch to remind me that I had been part of a brave and courageous unit; and, that part of life was finished.

Separated combatants produce better cease-fires.

February in Vietnam had the reputation of an action month. Vietnam's "Tet" holiday became synonymous with the war in February 1968 when the NVA-VC offensive resulted in a military win for America and a propaganda victory to the other side. A year later in 1969, we had a cease-fire during Tet that got started a bit later than planned. There had been talk of a holiday cease-fire in early February, but nothing developed so we were ordered out on canal ambush around dusk on the eve of Tet.

Around ten p.m., word came that a cease-fire beginning at midnight had been agreed to. This sounded like good news and we asked if the extraction helicopters were on the way. "Not tonight," was the reply. "We'll come out and get you tomorrow morning."

That's not what we wanted to hear. It was just like those rear echelon types to send us out knowing that a cease fire was in the works. Now we had to sit in paddy water up to our crotches all night while they drank beer and watched movies. What were we expected to do? Sit here and applaud when some gook boat floats past with supplies and ammo that will be used on us next week? A cease-fire means everyone stops whatever military activity is going on. Wonder how the VC get the cease fire message? Well, that's their problem not ours.

By midnight we were agreed that if the VC came floating by in a boat it was our duty to help them cease. Would this be violating the official cease-fire? Do we care? We're here, we're armed, we're wet and we aren't going to be extracted until tomorrow.

Maybe, in the spirit of the agreement, we should pull back from the canal into the big open dry rice paddy. That potentially endangers the team by exposing our position. And what would the gooks do if they heard us moving? Cease-fire? Don't think so. We would find out what a cease fire means to them. Anyway they probably won't know about a cease-fire until they read tomorrow's Stars and Stripes.

We hunker down and wait. Around two a.m. we hear the swish of something in the water. Sure enough, there's a boat moving down the canal, very quietly, no motor, riding the current. We're all on alert now. No one mentions a cease fire. One of the Rangers got anxious and clicked off a couple rounds. The boat hadn't come fully into the killing zone. We all opened up in a din of rifle, grenade and rocket fire mixed with shouts, screams, splashing and general ruckus.

It was over in two minutes. The disabled boat floated to the far bank of the canal so there was no way we could retrieve and search it. All we could do was shoot it up some more. We figured at least a couple VC got killed and one of their supply boats was now observing the cease-fire. We withdrew to the rice paddy for a better defensive position and waited for dawn extraction. Back home the company commander announced that the rest of the day's patrols were cancelled because we were honoring the cease fire. He congratulated us on a successful pre-cease-fire ambush.

Chopsticks work well for their intended purpose.

I learned to use chopsticks in Hong Kong. I went to Hong Kong on R&R in June 1969 because I had no knowledge about anything Chinese. I thought it would be fun to have a couple custom made suits and to buy Mao's Little Red Book and a Mao hat—items forbidden for sale in Vietnam. Because I grew up on a Kansas wheat farm, my knowledge of rice, the substance food for millions, was somewhat limited. Rice was shiny white and came out of a box. It was eaten in small quantities as a desert with sugar and milk. I wondered how so many Chinese could survive on that kind of diet.

Hong Kong would expand my knowledge and it sounded like a neat place to celebrate a 25th birthday. We went to the Fleet Club, the floating city, the New York Steak House, a noodle factory and the Royal Hong Kong Golf Club. In the New Territories we looked across a wide field and saw the inaccessible geography of Red China. For a Midwesterner it was pretty awesome and after five days, chopsticks were no longer enemy utensils. If not friends, they had become tolerable acquaintances. And you got an unexpected assist, because real Chinese rice sticks together.

Imposition may be opportunity.

The Company E Rangers moved north from Dong Tam to Tan An in July 1969. The Tan An base was a fraction of the size of Dong Tam so the Rangers were a bigger, more visible fish in a smaller pond. This meant additional responsibilities around camp including periodic perimeter guard duties, a function rotated among the Tan An units. It seemed to me that our Ranger "eliteness" combined with our emergency "on call" combat status made guard duty an imposition unworthy of the 75th. The cooks and clerks and other rear echelon types could handle the guard duty just fine—the threat of an attack was minimal. These other folks needed something to write home about, how they faced the enemy all night and kept him at bay. It would play well with their girl friends. We wouldn't have minded if the VC fired a few sniper rounds just to give them a taste of our routine.

So I let my team know that they had a bold leader (me) who would forcefully address the base command on the topic. I would make clear that perimeter guard duty constituted a misuse of the Ranger's time and skill. Our effectiveness in the field would surely be lessened from the fatigue and boredom of guard duty. Our operational rhythm of mission, rest day, preparation, mission, rest day, preparation, mission would be disrupted. Morale would collapse. Unit cohesion was threatened. Rangers would fight among themselves unless we were excused from the detail. I rehearsed with the team. A moment of silence fell. Someone said, "Hey, it's OK."

"What did you say?"

"It's OK. Don't worry about it."

"But two or three of you have to get out there tonight."

"We know that, no problem."

"You're volunteering?"

"Sure."

"And you don't mind?"

"No, there's plenty of guys willing."

"Without complaining and grousing?"

"No problem."

So I never had that conversation with the base commander. Ranger slots on the guard duty roster never went unfilled. I eventually understood that the guard posts, especially those in the 30-foot tower, had opportunities for social relaxation generally forbidden in the barracks area. Smoking special blends and the associated joking at the guard posts lay beyond the reaches of normal base restrictions and discipline. After all, it's Vietnam.

The Psalms are contemporary literature.

Other than a camera, the only personal item I took to Vietnam was a small Bible consisting of the New Testament and the Psalms. Over the year, with some regularity, I would read various Scriptures. The Psalms offered multiple examples of the Jewish authors' asking God why bad stuff like war happens. Where is God's hand in this awful situation? How is it that people who trust in God find themselves in worse conditions than "the heathen?" Writers of the Psalms questioned whether God saw and understood what was happening. And if so, how could God remain silent and fail to intervene?

The spirit of the Psalms seemed able to reach through millennia to touch 20th century combatants with language and emotions experienced by soldiers 3000 years earlier. At times angry, at times hopeless, at times desperate, at times dog tired, the Psalmists never abandoned faith in God's presence, whatever the condition. They declared with confidence that God's redemptive arm would, at the appointed time, extend to all people. The Psalms, many written by a soldier, became a spiritual anchor offering a sense of stability in an otherwise inexplicable amoral and chaotic situation over which no one seemed to have control.

Killing communists is easier if you don't see them.

Axiomatic to war is killing people and breaking things. Tragic as individual circumstances can be, there's a scar tissue around the reality that accepts killing as the cost of admission to combat. Possibly because of the reality and finality of death, the concept of killing other people rarely rests comfortably in any war discussion. One of the infantry training double-time chants went:

"I want to be an airborne ranger."

"I want to go to Vietnam."
"I want to be an airborne ranger."
"I want to kill some Viet Cong."

The words were less difficult if one thought of the Viet Cong as the foot soldiers for a totalitarian political philosophy imposed by force on unwilling recipients. The words were more problematic if one envisioned the Viet Cong as rice farmers, buffalo herders, fathers, brothers and sons. The sharper edges of killing other people are well obscured by military language. Combat photos normally avoid showing rows of bodies as evidence of success. Missions are designed to destroy the infrastructure, disrupt supply lines, take or reclaim territory, secure an area, defend a strategic point. The fact that people get killed in the course of these missions becomes incidental to the overall objective.

Perhaps the nature of the Vietnam war, one without well drawn lines of territorial dominance, ultimately led to the body count scorecard that came to appear in the daily headlines. By adding the numbers from the daily casualty report of dead and wounded Americans, Viet Cong, and South Vietnamese we developed a scorecard to measure military success and failure. Tragically, for neither America nor Vietnam did body counts determine the outcome, nor were those the measurements that mattered.

Shooting communists wasn't especially gratifying. Those I saw alive one moment and dead the next looked like most other Vietnamese I met in 1969 and afterward. If they had been wearing distinctive military uniforms, that might have made some difference. As it was these men likely had the same combat fears and intents as did the Rangers, except we were the ambush survivors.

As I sat on a wooden stool by a hooch one afternoon, a shot cracked and I heard the hiss of the passing bullet. Actually, I heard the hiss and the shot in that order. The sniper probably swore in Vietnamese when I didn't go down. We were frustrated that we weren't able to track him down, either.

On another day, we quietly moved inside a wood-line in what was known as a stay-behind mission. Half a dozen Rangers rode in with the helicopters extracting the infantry company. They silently offloaded as the infantrymen got on. Three hours later a VC patrol cautiously approached the area, probably looking for supplies or other paraphernalia the infantry troops discarded. The patrol walked right up to us. The problem was anxiety about opening fire too soon and missing. We didn't. They never fired back. Their war ended quickly.

Most of the VC we killed were ambushed. They were close enough for us to see, hear and count. We normally inflated the number of bodies on the assumption that we couldn't find every one we shot and others were probably wounded enough that they eventually died. More problematic was the captured weapons. Estimates of those weren't accepted. You had to produce the actual weapon because, (a) it could be easily hauled in, and (b) a captured weapon was one less available to be used against us. The system wasn't strict about correlating weapons with VC bodies. If we reported killing four VC but recovering no weapons, the report wasn't questioned. If four weapons were captured, it was easy to report twice that number of VC body count.

The captured weapons also made for great pictures; the standard photograph showed a Ranger team squatting behind a group of captured weapons spread on a display tarpaulin. Such photos, particularly showing multiple types of weapons, might be published in *Stars and Stripes*. The Rangers had other photos of the teams displaying dead VC. These were taken in the field, shared among the Rangers, but were not of publishing interest to the Army's Public Information Office.

One day at the PIO compound in Saigon I got to see a treasure of photos that were banned from publication. I particularly liked one, taken at Christmas 1968, showing two Army artillery Spec 4's dressed in Santa costumes standing by a howitzer. They held a 155 shell, brightly painted with green holly, red and white sugar canes and the greeting message: "Merry Christmas you VC bastards from your friends at the 113th Artillery Battery."

Whether a Vietnamese or an American soldier died, from a booby trap, from indirect artillery fire or from bombs dropped by aircraft operating at 30 thousand feet above the clouds, death can be held at some remote distance. For those who see the face of enemy or friend immediately before and after death, however, life and death are forever fused into eternal images.

Intelligence requires field verification

The Rangers often went on intelligence response missions. These included patrols to verify VC presence or mobilization, to search for supply or medical facilities, to locate weapons caches, to disrupt military planning meetings, and, most importantly, to do a "snatch." Of all the prizes valued by the U.S. brass, a captured VC or NVA officer ranked first. Therefore, intelligence reports of the location of these targets received immediate attention and action. I do not know of any successful snatch mission by Company E during 1969, but it wasn't for lack of trying. The Rangers had no reason to know the details of the intelligence reports, but were given fairly precise locations, time of the target's expected arrival and an estimate of the VC defensive capability. Within minutes of receiving the intelligence mission, we had our gear together and moved out.

While not returning with a snatch, we did discover every possible hole in the intelligence reporting. Sometimes the location was an open field at midday—an unlikely secret meeting site—or an uninhabited, inaccessible swamp area without trace of human presence, ever. Sometimes the location, a hooch, a house or a clearing, looked promising, but no one ever showed up for us to greet. One time we hit a hooch that had been used for some sort of gathering three or four days earlier. It was vacant and cold when we arrived although the intel folks were excited about our report. Despite some intelligence warnings of well guarded sites, we never ran into fire on these missions. They were useful as training exercises. At the same time I wondered if a different type of collaboration between those on the ground and the intelligence taskers would have improved the results.

Rangers were expected to supply intelligence as well as receive and act on it. We didn't do the supply side particularly well. First, no individualized or unit training in intelligence gathering, requirements or reporting was provided. Post mission intelligence debriefings normally involved a conversation between the team leader only and the unit's designated intelligence officer. The conversation was little more than an oral, chronological trip report rather than a professional debriefing. Little feedback was given to the teams on the intelligence that might have had some value. From time to time we heard in the troop grapevine that an artillery mission or a bombing run had been called because of our reporting. No one gave it much thought at the time.

Intelligence channels did provide us some experimental equipment for field trials. The "starlight" scopes, first generation hand carried night vision enhancement devices, proved themselves exceptionally effective in upgrading our night operating capabilities. The scopes had two drawbacks that were related to limitations of the current state of the technical art: (a) the scopes were heavy and bulky, and (b) they were not very effective during the five days of each month on either side of the new moon, particularly under cloudy conditions. Since the scopes were new, availability was limited and not every team had one for every mission. Increasingly through 1969, however, the teams learned to use and rely on the starlight's visual advantage. By the latter part of the year, my team moved with great confidence throughout the darkest night hours. We had partially taken back the night from the VC by being able to "see" otherwise obscured and unfamiliar terrain; and, like the VC, to use the cover of night to our advantage.

By contrast most Ranger teams found little value in the new generation of perimeter sensors. The sensor arrays had been developed to expand the defensive perimeter of a unit. Rangers were haunted by the potential for the VC to sneak up on a team in its nighttime position. However, if movement sensors could be placed at some distance on the team's perimeter, the presence of anyone approaching the team could be detected and preparation made for the intruder. The seriousness of early warning from the teams had been reinforced in January 1969 when a Company E team was virtually wiped out by a surprise assault on their night position.

We tried the sensor perimeter alert system three or four times before abandoning the equipment. The sensors were lightweight enough. They reliably picked up and conveyed movement. For Ranger deployment, however, the shortcomings became quickly apparent.

First, placement and retrieval proved cumbersome. Attention to detail while placing the sensor was required for optimum performance. Direction, relative dryness, and stability of device were all important. Placing the sensor after dark, the preferred time for a team to set up, required more personnel movement, commotion and potential location compromise than acceptable. Retrieval of the sensors, particularly if the team wanted to reposition itself during the night demanded more movement and time. Repositioning, an action normally based on some need for a rapid, quick, stealth movement, was largely incompatible with retrieving, disassembly and re-packing the sensor array.

Secondly, the sensors were indiscriminate in detecting movement. Water buffalo, wind, ducks, critters, and civilians as well as VC would trigger the sensor. If the devices were close enough to the team that the cause of such movement could be observed, they were too close to do much good. If far enough away to provide early warning, the "false" or "benign" warnings distracted attention and created unduly heightened anxiety. The Rangers quickly abandoned technology that didn't work reliably in the field operating environment.

Trust the front line.

The man in the field possesses the wisdom of Solomon when his welfare is at stake. The Rangers collectively had little more than a high school education. They were, nevertheless, acutely self aware of their responsibilities, strengths and limitations. The mission, responsibilities, dangers, risks and interdependence were either quickly understood and accepted, or one got out. One day a career E-6 who wasn't a regular member of my team volunteered to go out with us because we were a man light. He had a couple tours under his belt and seemed like a capable fellow. Another member of the team objected because the E-6 was "a crazy bastard." However, I wanted a full team so I dismissed the concern.

After we were on the ground I learned that, in addition to his water canteen, the E-6 always carried a flask of fine whiskey. He didn't save it to treat snake bites. Several hours into the mission, as feared, the E-6 did start acting crazy. He "smelled gooks" and began throwing grenades randomly at the scent. He heard them "crawling up on us." He imagined being surrounded. He got completely out of control to the point that he became dangerous to us all. We got help from the command, who pulled us out early. Back at camp, members of the team let me know that if they ever went on another mission with the E-6, he would likely be a casualty. The company commander didn't risk the obvious and the man left the Rangers.

The Rangers prized stealth, flexibility and movement over official doctrine about personal survival. Among the standard combat gear issuances that were immediately discarded by Rangers were steel pots, flack jackets and the entrenching tool. Besides weight, a constant enemy for Rangers who needed to move quietly was noise, particularly metal on metal. Such sounds could be heard over great distances in the still Vietnam night. Steel pots and entrenching tools had both steel and weight problems. The flack jackets were heavy, bulky and hot. As the Company E method of operation was move, hide, hit, move, hide and hit again, few had use for protective gear. The Rangers opted for low maintenance, light, small offensive weapons and equipment. They knew what worked for them in the field and discarded the rest.

Ranger teams understood interdependence. Mission preparation appeared unstructured, but individual team members planned among themselves the quantities and distribution of grenades, weapons, water, insect repellent, ammunition, food, maps, communications gear, explosives and the like. The rehearsal ritual—with everybody saddled up in full gear and camouflage before getting on the helicopter—involved vigorous jumping up and down to detect any clanging or rattling from equipment or poorly packed ruck sacks. If noise was heard, no command was necessary to initiate re-pack. All understood the shared stake in mission success.

The E-4's and E-5's may have sensed the eventual futility of America's Vietnam policy earlier and with more sophisticated reasoning than the U.S. protestors or the VC's international propagandists. The Rangers and their infantry counterparts quickly understood the war was not the uprising of indigenous South Vietnamese. They understood the war was a fully sponsored effort by the North whose interest was to "unify" Vietnam by any means necessary under the North's one party government. While many quietly questioned whether the American effort was worth the cost, they chose to subordinate personal opinion to the collective judgment of America's political and military leadership. They accepted an obligation to their country in military service knowing the risk and the absence of reward. Certainly some Rangers found personal identity in combat and its associated brutality and bravery. But their conversations normally centered on the temporary job they had been given to do. The Rangers were as much bemused as angry by highly publicized actions of American celebrities who consorted with the enemy in ways that shamed American values and promoted disunity. They understood what the rest of the world would eventually learn—the NVA and the VC were not the good guys. The best that could be said was North and South Vietnamese shared a cultural history. At the insistence of the North, the rifle, not the ballot, was deciding how that history would enter the 21st century. America's trust was well placed with these 20 year-old patriotic realists who respected the country's call to duty.

Tough times make us laugh.

I went to one of Bob Hope's Christmas shows in December 1969. Thousands of GI's milled around the outdoor stage for three or four hours in 90-degree sun awaiting the performance. I don't recall the punch lines or the musical titles but I never enjoyed an event more—before or after. The women were beautiful and charming. The musicians were auditioning for the heavenly choir. Johnny Bench won my Hall of Fame vote. Bob Hope made me believe this show was the pinnacle of his career. All cynicism I had about the USO and its "morale building mission", disappeared. If Bob Hope had spoken Vietnamese that day, all the VC and NVA would have defected.

There was the night when word circulated among the Rangers that a lady willing to provide carnal entertainment had been able to sneak by the MP's at the main gate. Reportedly the show would begin around nine p.m. at a secret location. To know the location would cost you $5. The marketing campaign sold out and ticket holders were advised to bring additional cash as, with proper encouragement, the evening could evolve into an audience participation performance art show. Another $5 was assessed at the door. As it turned out, for $10 (Ranger pay was about $7 per day) the audience got to watch a not quite naked dancer perform a Vietnamese interpretation of the "go-go." The show ended when the entertainer's mother put a curfew on her daughter and restricted the act to no contact. The promoter's reputation suffered terribly.

The Tan An commander decided to clean up the base. My Ranger team was on stand-down between missions, so we got the duty. General grumbling followed. This would be a long day in the hot sun. Scraps of this and that, plus accumulated litter and trash had to be picked up, then hauled to the dump and unloaded. After that, the Vietnamese locals would pick through the trash for items of use. The day wasn't starting off well at all.

"Sarge," yelled out a Ranger we called Tex, "do we have a truck?"

"I think we can get one if we need it."

"Then let's do the whole camp."

"What? Are you still smoking weed?"

"No, listen to me." I told the commander we would do the whole camp if we could have a truck. He was happy to oblige.

Tex assumed command. For the next ten hours a happy crew of Rangers roamed Tan An base loading trash and any other unsecured material that we could lift into the truck. Plywood, corrugated tin, plastic containers, lumber, wire, crates, boxes, ammo cases, all had to be cleaned up. We would load the truck in about two hours, head for the dump and return for another load.

Challenged by those in non-Ranger areas who asked what we were doing we responded, "Didn't you get the word? The old man declared this "Camp clean up day", and since the Rangers are always getting exempted from base duties, he is making us do this for everyone." Many said thanks.

When the truck headed for the dump, we took a side street. There Tex knew someone who knew some locals involved in private sector construction. As a result the Rangers became involved in the export business, providing surplus American goods to foreign buyers, thereby supporting the Tan An civilian economy. Our production costs approached zero and Uncle Sam covered transportation expenses. Thus, the selling price of the lumber, tin, wooden crates and all other items on each truckload could be negotiated fairly quickly. It was a hard, sweaty, smelly day for sure, but the camp never looked more orderly than when we finished. The commander expressed appreciation for the positive, volunteer spirit we displayed. I said we would be willing to do it again in three months. We each made an extra month's salary for the effort.

Insertion into a landing zone at the beginning of a mission raised anxiety and tension to peak level. As the Huey's descended rapidly, the Rangers looked for any movement, listened for fire and prepared to step off the skids at the instant of touchdown. It was the most dangerous point in a mission for both the helicopter pilots and Rangers.

Insertion points were always considered "enemy" territory with the possibility of meeting a lead and steel reception committee. Procedures said the skids should touch the ground before off loading, Rangers would move at least ten feet away from the helicopter and go prone on the ground as cover for hostile fire. If we took fire we would be supported by gunships, but the Huey may not be able to get back down for an extraction. We feared off-loading into a mine field or a punji pit emplacement; and, on occasion aborted insertions because of those.

One day we approached an open LZ of paddies near a hamlet that we intended to search. Reportedly, the VC used this as a resupply location so we expected to find stores of rice and other necessities of life. Many of the paddies were flooded, but a hundred meters from the hamlet were a couple of unplanted areas where I directed the pilot. We were prepared for a hot LZ due to intelligence about the area, but didn't take any fire on approach. Nevertheless, I wanted off the chopper fast and told the pilot, "We're jumping off the skids before you touch ground. We need to get down and you need to get out of here."

"Roger that."

Eighteen inches above the ground six Rangers simultaneously jumped off the skids. Under max thrust the Huey pulled out.

There had been no visible water in the landing surface. No one considered the fact that surface water usually didn't collect in diked holding areas that served to amass and store the organic fertilizer used on the paddies where the rice is planted.

Six Rangers touched the surface together and six Rangers sank ankle, knee, thigh and crotch deep in a pool of human and animal excrement. Stuck, the Rangers were like silhouettes on the target range. Nearly waist deep in the muck, movement was virtually impossible. Weapons were held high and cursing was heard. But there was no fire; the LZ was cold.

Methodically the Rangers began to pull one another through the sewage, one holding the rifle of the next to gain sufficient leverage for movement. The stench was awful. The chopper pilots found reason for immediate amusement that wasn't shared by the Rangers for several hours.

There was a Ranger who, in applying his camouflage, always completely blackened his face. Then, with the green stick, he drew a circle encompassing his forehead, cheeks and chin. Staying with the green he drew an upside down Y running from the top of his forehead down the bridge of his nose and angled the legs of the Y to the corners of his mouth and intersecting with the circle. He wanted the VC to know he came in peace.

The Rules of War

by Jack Bick

There have been many attempts to have rules for war. War is barbaric and any attempt to civilize it with rules is destined to failure. While the concept is laudable and logical, it pales in the stark light of actual warfare.

Vietnam brought this home to many through the highly publicized My Lai incident. I cannot speak for the conscience of Lieutenant Calley. However, there is no doubt in my mind that rules did not apply to many situations that I encountered in Vietnam.

The VC were adept at moving supplies and war materiel in small shipments carried by a few individuals within a region. If the materiel were to go a longer distance, they would be passed along to other "mules" in a daisy chain. This allowed for efficient movement of supplies without being detected because each person in the chain knew their territory and where the Americans were set up.

One evening a small group of soldiers were flown into an area just south of the Mekong River. It was suspected that supplies were being transported through this area by locals. There were only a few hooches in the area of dense jungle vegetation, a perfect place to secret supplies during the day for transport at night.

Twelve of us landed and quickly set about securing the area. My main function was to gather information for a story and take photographs for the division newspaper. Until the area was secure I considered my primary duty to be just another fighting man and to be ready to defend myself.

Ten of the soldiers were from a line unit of the 9th Infantry Division. As such they carried M-16s, a few grenades, two men also carried grenade launchers. There was one lieutenant and one radio man. Most of these men wore flack jackets and steel helmets for this mission.

The lieutenant was young—weren't they all. He was nervous because he was not accustomed to having this small of a unit surrounding him. We slowly moved into the hooch area where we found the inhabitants to be open to our presence.

The usual females and children were there, plus one military age male. He claimed to be an ARVN soldier home on leave and produced the papers to verify that fact. The lieutenant was still uncertain so he assigned a private to follow the man and keep him in the area. The other soldiers searched the thatched hooches for hidden bunkers, ratholes and weapons. None were found so everyone was positioned to guard the perimeter.

The youngest women was frying fish heads and rice for dinner and offered some to those of us who set up in her hooch. We ate since it wasn't sundown yet and we could not set up for our mission until full darkness.

Once dinner was over and the woman had cleaned up the dented metal plates, she gathered the children and put them to bed.

The bed consisted of bamboo strapped together to form a frame on legs. Reeds were strapped across the frame and a mat filled with tree palms served as a mattress. The bed was about the size of a double bed in America.

The woman and the man then turned out the flames in the two lanterns and retired for the night in the same bed with the children. With limited light there is no reason to stay up.

At full darkness we quietly left the hooches to set up at the end of a clearing near where the "sniffers" detected movement the previous night thought to be the supply line.

The eleventh man in the unit was an American Indian from northern New York. He was round faced and built with great bulk in the neck and shoulders. Great pains had been taken to keep him away from the hooches because he was a "sniper."

"Snipers" I was told were against the Geneva Convention. But both sides, nevertheless, used them in Vietnam. The sniper with this team of soldiers was employed as a way to get close to the supply line without spooking the enemy into inactivity. He carried an M-14 fitted with a starlight scope for night vision.

The line troops set up behind the "sniper" to guard the flanks and rear of our position. This was a waiting game in complete silence. The locals knew we were in the area but they were asleep when we left the hooches and we did not proceed in a direct line to the ambush site,

After hours of waiting, patience paid off. The silence cracked with the explosion from the rifle of the sniper, a slight pause and then two quick additional rounds were sent to the target, one of them a tracer round that marked the trajectory with a red line.

Then silence. We all waited for an attack or the sound of retreat from the area. None came. We waited until first light to recon the area.

The "sniper" hit three for three. Two had struggled several yards into the jungle, but the wounds were right to the heart. The third kill dropped at the point of contact. The back of the body was just a massive bloody hole. The rifleman flipped the body over on its back. There lay the woman who fed us dinner the night before. On either side of her were bundles of uniforms, sandals, medicine and ammunition—care packages for enemy soldiers.

The shooter ripped open her black pajama blouse to expose her graying skin with a bullet hole just to the right of center between her small brown nipples. There was burnt flesh around the wound from the tracer bullet.

Her husband was one of the other bodies. Earlier in the evening they presented themselves as allies. But in truth, they were the enemy. In such a war can any soldier consider anyone to be an ally at any point in time? The answer is, "No, not if you want to live."

The training and experience were enough to make precaution the word of the day, every day. On one operation with a line unit of approximately 80 infantrymen, we swept an area that had a rather large village by Mekong Delta standards. The village was deserted but had been inhabited within the last 24 hours. Fires had recently died away. Clothes were still hanging out to dry and food remained on tables, yet cold. In the middle of the compound was a colorful metal Viet Cong flag.

No one would approach it for fear that it was booby trapped. It was too obvious, practically the only color in the village among all the earth tones of the thatch hooches, dirt and black clothing.

As the soldiers fanned out through the village to check each hooch for occupants, bunkers and ratholes, one Gomer Pyle looking individual forgot every word of his Basic and Combat training and approached the metal flag. Someone screamed "NO!!!" as he bent to retrieve the unique souvenir.

The cries did no good as his hand cupped to pick it up. Everyone, who was aware of his action, took a step away and started to crouch. As he stood up with the brightly colored metal flag we were all surprised when nothing happened. The damned thing had not been booby-trapped.

Two thoughts ran through my mind almost simultaneously, "What a great souvenir," and "the gooks missed a great opportunity to kill some Americans."

Everyone breathed a sigh of relief and each shared at least one of my concerns. The sweep continued without incident. The VC had been spooked by something and we found no trace of them within a klick of the village.

Despite the lost opportunity for that flag, my sense of precaution continued.

Once you were aware that everyone was the enemy, or at least was potentially the enemy, you became more aware of what was happening around you.

Every base had Vietnamese who came into the compound to clean, wash clothes and shine boots. If you watched them carefully when they moved from barrack to barrack, quite often they would be pacing off the steps. These calculations would later become coordinates for mortar attacks. The next day none of the mamasans would show up for work for fear of retribution, especially if there were American casualties.

No one ever went into the town to find these enemies and kill them for giving information to the enemy—but we would have been justified. The problem, especially in the Delta, the home of the Viet Cong movement, we would have to kill everyone to stop the killing of our soldiers. Either directly or out of fear, or just complicity, everyone was on the other side from us.

Yet we had to interact with the gooks even though we knew they were the enemy. This is what creates a "bunker mentality". This is what creates tension, and tension creates mistakes and over reaction. Movies like "Platoon" look real, but they are no different than cartoons compared to the real situation in Vietnam and what each person experienced.

I'm sure the gooks felt the same way. "What are these Americans doing here? We can take care of ourselves. Why are they killing us, we just want to live our simple lives? Who cares about the politicians in Saigon and Washington?" I'm sure they were left with a bunker mentality, too.

This is the same situation we have today in our inner cities between the police and the citizens. As the old song says, "...the answer my friend is blowin in the wind, when will we ever learn?"

As an Army journalist I had the opportunity to move around the country and to visit Saigon a number of times. The capital city was a decaying European city with a replica of the Cathedral of Notre Dame at the end of a street canopied by trees. At the other end was a bustling downtown where the French Opera Hall had been turned into the home of the legislative body of the country. The Hall was flanked on one side by the Caravel Hotel where most of the civilian press lived. On the opposite side was the Continental Hotel, where more foreign intrigue occurred than Rick's American Café in Casablanca.

Just down TuDo Street were the shops frequented by the wives and children of the officials of the ruling regime who were really profiting from the war—silk dresses for the women and sophisticated toys of the day for the children. This was all in contrast to the suffering on both sides outside of Saigon where the war really happened.

While the war proved to me that I did have inner strength, I was disillusioned by the futility of it all. While I gained inner confidence that I could stand up to pressure, I felt powerless to make a difference there.

Survival was the key. Live through the year, get back to the World, my mother and my future wife, Angie.

There was a certain resignation to the ever present saying, "Kill them all and let God sort them out."

The Bo Bo Canal

by Paul A. Newman

Fred sipped his wine. He had added ice to it which resulted in condensation that dripped in his lap. He hated that, but it was too hot not to drink with ice.

He watched the birds flit down from branch to branch before they reached the bird feeders. A small red squirrel scratched at the bay feeder and spilled seed all over the ground. Blue jays, crackles, and doves kept their distance from each other as they pecked at the bounty showered on them.

Bob, his son, came onto the screened in porch. Fred glanced at him, watched him sit at his right side. His son, soon to be gone. A blessing and a curse. Off to college, finally. Out of high school, finally. But he was a good kid, most of the time. The mouth on that kid. Where did he get it? Did I treat my parents like that? What's with these kids today? Too soft. They needed a war like we had. Yes, like we had.

"Dad!" said Bob, looking intently at Fred.

Fred switched his gaze slowly to his son. "Bob,…what?"

"Dad, it's time, you know."

"Ok, go cut the lawn then. Although it doesn't look like it needs it." Humor gets them every time.

"Dad, it's time. Not the lawn. It's time you told me about the war. Remember, you said when I was eighteen you would tell me about the war. You said I wasn't old enough before. Eighteen was the magic age. Now I'm eighteen. Let's hear it."

"Probably not a good time, son. I'm on my second glass of wine."

"Yeah, sure. Probably the best time, don't you think?" Bob had seen him drink before. He'd finish the entire bottle in less than two hours. At least he was wise enough in his stuporous state not to drive. Never got a DUI.

"Dad, when is a good time? Now's as good as any. I'm leaving for college in a week. When? I ask. When is a good time? This is as good as any. Mom's shopping and Mary is out riding her stupid horse."

"Yes, that is one stupid horse." Fred drawled. "Ahh, what the hell. A story or two won't hurt. Might help a little. Been awhile since I've even thought about it."

"Well, you've never talked about it with me. And I never heard you talk about it with anyone else, except that guy in DC. What's his name? Wallace?"

"Bob Wallace. Yeah, the governor, we talked about some things once. Not much though. And Jack Bick, too. Not something you talk about too freely, you know."

"Dad, I don't know. That's why I'm asking you now that it is time to share with your son some parts of yourself. The war. It was thirty years ago. Don't you think your son should know what you did in the war?"

Fred commiserated with himself. He stared as the over heavy drops of condensation rolled down the side of his wine glass, combined together and dropped on his pants leg. He saw, but he did not see. Bob watched him.

A minute passed. Another minute. Bob watched without saying a word.

"There was the Bo Bo Canal. I hated that fucking mosquito ridden place," he paused. Took a sip of wine. "The Bo Bo Canal. It was a canal as straight as an arrow. Twenty miles long, at least. Never measured it. Saw it from the air, straight. Built by the French. Straight Frogs. Then there was one bend in it several miles before it went into the river. Better than a road. A water road it was."

Fred stopped. After several minutes, Bob prodded him.

"So, tell me about the Bo Bo Canal. What did you do there? Where was it—where is it?"

"Well, I guess it's time you learned a story or two. When I used to have to listen to my dad about his war stories, he bored me to tears. Man, he wouldn't shut up about them. But that was the big one—WWII. Not our war," he paused again. "Ok, Bob, I'll tell you a story about the war. I don't like to talk about it much, especially with people who know and care nothing about it, but I will. Let me fill up my glass first."

Fred proceeded to the kitchen, added ice to the oversized red wine glass, poured in almost half a bottle of Chateau Neuf du Pape—a nice dark red, good color, good taste. He had been drinking red wine for twenty-five years. But now the wine he bought was expensive. His taste had matured to the wines that cost over twenty-five dollars a bottle. Only on Fridays and Saturdays would he indulge himself. And they were good wines. Luckily, neither his wife nor children followed his habit.

Fred eased himself into the chair, put his feet up on the ottoman, sipped his wine. Glanced at the birds.

"You missed a Baltimore Oriole."

"You didn't call me?"

"It would have spooked him anyways."

"Damn, I haven't seen one this summer, yet. Had an Evening Grosbeak last night. First one in about six years. I would have liked to see the Oriole. But that famous Baltimore Oriole, or should I say craven raven, Art Modell, the terror of the town of Cleveland can still go to hell. Hah!" Fred imitated spitting.

"The war, Dad."

"Yes, yes, we're getting to it. Can't rush a good thing, you know. It's only been thirty years since the war. I have to assemble my thoughts. Not easy at this age."

"You're only fifty."

"Yes,' he spoke softly, "only fifty. "And the war was thirty years ago. Seems like just yesterday. But I don't think I could carry all that weight with me now."

"What weight?"

"What weight? Jesus, son. Let me tell you about the weight. When I carried the machine gun, the M-60, it alone weighed thirty-five pounds. Four bandoliers of ammunition was an additional thirty pounds. Then a pistol and five cartridges in case the gun jammed and I was without a weapon, that was another five pounds. Then food for several days, add another three pounds. Then clean water, two canteens, another three or four pounds. I hated to add iodine to the water. Always knew I would get kidney problems or something from so much iodine. But it kept those little bugs from getting a hold of the inside of me."

"Then we each had to carry two smoke grenades, another five pounds. Then four regular grenades, another five pounds. Then a williepeter or two, that's white phosphorous. We used them to burn hootches. Couldn't put out one of those fires. Then a flashlight, compass, knife taped upside down to the shoulder harness for easy accessibility. Mosquito repellent. Ugh, those mosquitos. Must be the national bird in Vietnam, the mosquito."

"The weight. Must have been seventy, eighty pounds sometimes. You step in the mud and you stay there. You just sink And we carried other shit, just don't remember it all. Amazing what I don't remember."

"Well, if you never talk about it, how are you going to remember it? Mr. Randles, the history teacher, says you will forget most things you learn unless you repeat them periodically. If you don't talk about something for thirty yeas, what do you expect."

Fred smiled. "Don't get flip, son. I remember."

"Ok, dad, the Bo Bo whatever? Let's hear about the Bo Bo," he pronounced Bo Bo in low tones as if he was calling a dog.

"All right, the Bo Bo Canal. What a mission." He hesitated a moment. "Let me organize my thoughts for a second or two.

"I had been in country for about seven months, the team leader of team 2-1, a Staff Sergeant, at that. Twenty years old and a Staff Sergeant. That was big stuff. I could go into the PX and buy hard liquor. Couldn't do that in civilian life, but as a Staff Sergeant, I could and did. Sometimes too much, but that's another story for another day. I'll try not to ramble too much like my father did. Try not to bore you too much here."

"So the captain tells me we have another mission on the Bo Bo Canal. That I have to do an overflight at noon. That is where you go in a helicopter or a little bird dog plane and fly over the area to see where you are going to insert for the ambush. The Bo Bo Canal is in the Plain of Reeds. It is just that, a plain of reeds and water. A canal had been dug by the French for transportation through the Plain of Reeds. It was a wonderful canal except for the fact that we had to lay next to it all night with the mosquitos. Luckily we sometimes found a high spot so we weren't laying in the water. Even water in eighty degree weather gets cold after four hours. And the wrinkles on your skin—you couldn't move after that."

"So, I get to the helipad for the flyover, I think it was the helipad, you know, I can't remember if the flyover was a plane or a helicopter. Just don't remember. Probably not a significant point. What is significant, is that I don't remember. There were so many flyovers with both bird dogs and helicopters. But I do remember seeing the troops on the ground. There was a platoon spread over about three hundred meters protecting the sniffer boys. These guys were burying movement detectors. They would bury these electronic devices at various so called strategic points which would send out a radio signal if there was movement. In this manner, the intelligence authorities could send us in for an ambush if there was significant movement. Where they were burying this stuff, no one walked. It was in the middle of the Plain of Reeds. But who knows, I was just a grunt, so I never had access to the info they got. We just went where we were sent."

"We flew the Bo Bo. I got an impression of where I wanted to go in. Pointed it out to the pilot, he wrote it down on his map. They would then direct the troops to make their way to that point for extraction later in the day. We were a stay behind mission. The gooks would see the troops they had been watching all day get extracted and they would think things were all clear. However, with our camouflage, we would sneak off the helicopter as the troops got on the helicopter. Then, we would lay low for a long time to make sure the gooks knew the troops were gone. They would use the canal for transportation. If we were lucky, we would catch them transporting something.

"The big trouble…"

"Dad, can I have a glass of wine?" Interrupted Bob.

"Nice try, son. No. On second thought, why not. Get yourself a small glass of wine. Sure, what the hell. Maybe we'll get drunk together. Won't your mother be pleased! Look at them, both drunk and he's telling war stories. Jeez!"

Bob put his glass on the small table next to the chair. He used little ice, thinking to capitalize on the volume of wine.

"Ok, dad, the Bo Bo," this time he said it as Boo boo, again in low tones. Did he know Yogi Bear and 'Hey, Boo Boo' of Jellystone Park? He was too young. That was the sixties.

"Oh yes, the big trouble with the canal is, was, that sometimes the gooks would send one or two sampans ahead of the major transport column. So if you attacked the first one or two sampans, you were subjecting yourself to being attacked and swarmed over by the rest of the gooks. And there was no where to run to. The Plain of Reeds, you could see for a mile. It was flat, wet, and reedy. So you had to try to get a spot that allowed you to see as far as you could see to determine if you were going to attack the first sampan.

"But we usually didn't have that problem. I had been to the Bo Bo Canal four or five times and nothing had ever come along except hordes of mosquitos; and, an occasional leech. So we did the overflight, I selected the insert location. We were going in about five-thirty that evening. We looked forward to a night of nothing but mosquitos.

"We were operating out of an area called Tan An. We had moved from an area south of Saigon about ninety miles, called Dong Tam, to an area about twenty-three miles south of Saigon called Tan An. The war was winding down. Nixon was consolidating. Troops were being sent home and not replaced. Units were getting smaller. The political feeling back home, according to Time Magazine, which, by the bye, we read assiduously, was that the country was tired of their boys being killed for a bunch of gooks. In retrospect, we allowed a communist government to take control of millions of minds. Like a vise on the head. But those weren't my decisions. Nixon was catering to the populace that elected him and that was that. The crook was a good politician. But Melvin Laird can still kiss my ass. But that again is another story for another time. He was the Cabinet Member in charge of defense, Secretary of Defense. He couldn't even be my secretary, now. Pompous, self important, piece of shit, as far as I'm concerned. Not a real troop on the ground supporter...."

"The Bo Bo, Dad, get to the point, Dad."

"Yeah, yeah. You waited eighteen years for this shit, you can take it as it comes. Stream of consciousness. Wasn't that a medium for novels for the longest time? D.H. Lawrence, James Joyce—you know, you've read all those, haven't you?" Fred snickered. Sure, his kid, read—fat chance.

"Whatever flows from your mind in a stream. Ok, don't look at me like your mother does. The Bo Bo. We're getting to it." He sipped, more liked gulped, a swallow of wine. Good wine.

"So, we had to get ready. We had an area where we put everything. You know, I can't remember specifically the area we assembled at Tan An. At Dong Tam it was by the supply shack on the picnic tables and the sandbags surrounding the supply shack and bar. But for the life of me, I can't remember where we assembled at Tan An. Doesn't matter does it? But the process of assembly was a ritual. Get all your gear together. Put all your camoflage on. Make sure all your stuff was noiseless. We, I, would have the guys get their gear on and jump up and down to make sure there was no jingling. I remember Durkin. What a jingler he was, good guy, but a jingler. More noise you never heard. You could have him noiseless when he went out, but he was still noisy. But he wasn't on my team at that time. I think he made the noise to scare the gooks away. I wanted no noise so the gooks wouldn't know we were there."

"But these guys on my team, this group was good. They had been with me for awhile and they were noiseless. Good at hand signals, they loved the camouflage. Booth used to always put his on a certain way. He had streaks from his cheeks. We all thought we were Indians painting up for the big war party. But it was effective. You couldn't see a ranger in the woods unless he moved."

"Let me tell you about the men on that mission. If I can remember their names. It was so long ago, and so many missions. Let's see, there was Booth, I told you about how he put on the camouflage. He seemed to be the youngest. I was twenty years old, he had to be nineteen. He seemed so much younger than us. He was still a spec four at that time. Don't even remember where he came from, but he had been on my team for months. He was a good field man.

"Then there was Konovalov, the Russian. He was American, but of Russian descent, so we called him 'the Russian'. He was tall, but then, everyone was taller than me. I'm only five foot six and a half inches, so everyone seems taller. But Konov was tall. And no one was fat. They were all lean, muscular, strong young men. Konov and Booth were buddies. They seemed to do things together. I wonder if they keep in contact with each other? Who knows. It'd be interesting to see them talk about those times.

"I also had Koenig on my team. Now he was a character. He was a Staff Sergeant, outranked me in time in grade. Mine was a field grade, but he had been a Staff Sergeant for several years. He was a Staff Sergeant when he came into the company. It caused some problems because of the army respect, sometimes unduly, for rank. Doesn't matter if you are the dumbest shit in the world, if you outrank someone, you are the boss. And that was the situation with Koenig until it settled down. They put him as assistant team leader for a while. Then, somehow, he got deposited with my team, because the other teams either didn't work well with him, or he wouldn't take instructions from them, or some conflict. He wasn't even my assistant team leader, just a member on the team. He was funny. He had a way of rolling up his eyelids so the pink part showed. He would do it for pictures, or come up to you with his eyelids rolled back and ask a serious question."

"But the good one was for the group picture we took. The developed photo showed Koenig standing on the end of the group of guys and his dick was hanging out, exposed. What a great shot. He looked so serious, all the guys looked like tough rangers and here's this guy with his dick hanging out. What a picture. I still have that picture. I'll show it to you someday."

"Let's see, then I had my assistant team leader, Moseley. He was from New Hampshire, I think. He was our karate expert. Loved to kick. Apparently had training in it. Saw him kick a prisoner one day, that gook went sprawling. Wish I knew what the gook said, but we only knew some swear words, or 'di di mau', or 'la dai'—git or stop. I still can't for the life of me figure out why the military doesn't teach the local language to the troops. If we're to be there for a year, we could have communicated with the people a lot better. Might have saved a number of lives. But we didn't know the language. Strange.

"Moseley, dark hair, probably five-nine or ten, broad shouldered. I wrote to his girlfriend's girlfriend, had a correspondence with her for months. Even wrote after the war for awhile, but then it just drifted away, like a lot of things. Just drifts away.

"Dad, are we ever going to get to the Bo Bo?"

"See, I told you, I'm going to be just like my own father, boring as hell. I have to give you the background on these guys so you know how they interact on the mission. How they interacted with me, the team leader. Just relax. It's only a story. You've got a little wine, I see you have an empty glass. Go fill it, but don't tell your mother you had two glasses. And don't drink it so fast. You've got to sip it, savor it, enjoy it. It's not a like the beer you sneak where you chug it with your friends. Go ahead."

Fred sipped while Bob dispensed with the wine glass and got a water glass, put some ice in it and filled it with wine.

Fred looked at the water glass. "I see you're cheating."

"I didn't like that glass."

"Yup. I bet you didn't," he chuckled. "So back to Moseley, the kicker. He had been on my team ever since I got one. Good troop. Screwed up one time, let a prisoner get away from him. We crossed a log bridge, Moseley was last. When the gook got over, he ran at a right angle like hell into the woods. Mosely couldn't shoot for fear of hitting us and he was balanced on the log so he couldn't get his balance to shoot. And he had his gun on safety so he couldn't just blow him away. The gook was gone. Boy, was I pissed. And boy-o-boy, was Moseley embarrassed. Then the next time, not trusting Moseley to walk the gook, I took him in front of me. And, strange as it may seem, he ran. But I'm off safe, I put twenty rounds into his torso before he got twenty feet away. Sucker was still alive with that look of fear in his face as I stood over him. Needless to say, he was dispensed with. I was so pissed at that gook! Running away with a gun in your back. Of all the brass balls!"

"But Moseley was good. He learned from that mistake. As assistant, we worked well together.

"Then there was Mex. He wasn't Mexican, but he was from New Mexico, so we called him Mex. He was one crazy son of a bitch. One of the best men to have on your team in a firefight, but one crazy son of a bitch. I mean crazy.

"Just a small side-light story on Mex. He was maybe an inch taller than me, very very broad shouldered and extremely strong. A friendly guy. What a sense of humor. But don't piss him off—he was strong, and, he was crazy. I don't even remember how he got on my team, but he was an asset in the field, if, and I say that cautiously, if he could be controlled.

"One time he was in a fight at the company area in Dong Tam. There was another guy, Campbell, who was bigger than Mex, but a little flabbier. Campbell had an attitude. He talked to you like he was superior. That you were just dog shit. He was from the New Jersey area, had that accent. And he went to college for a couple of years, so obviously, that made him better than the rest of us. And of course, better than me because I had flunked out of college after one semester. But he wasn't a team leader, only an assistant on another team. But he thought he was superior. Mex wouldn't buy it. He just didn't give a shit. So people started to surmise who would win a fight between the two of them. Most took the side of Mex because they liked him. He was an extremely likable fellow. But it was a toss up to look at them."

"Dad, aren't we getting to the Bo Bo Canal at some time here?" asked Bob.

"Yes, we are. But we are getting there in a roundabout way. Consider this the overflight. I am giving you a view of the area first. And slow down on drinking that wine. This isn't the feast of Cana, it's not water turned to wine, you know."

"Yeah, sure Dad. I know how to drink wine. I've watched you drink enough of it."

"Whoa son. I think maybe that wine is getting to you. Back off. You wanted to hear this shit, so sit back and let it roll."

"Sorry."

Fred hesitated, scrutinizing the situation. Was his son getting drunk with him sitting right there? Did he really want to hear these old stories? Oh, this memory lane. Just thinking about it—like I was right there. Well, we'll tell him this one about the Bo Bo and leave it at that. But I'm sure going to tell it my way. It's my memory, fading as it is.

"So the boys, that's anybody around, and especially Old Frosty—that's another E-6 who had been around a long time—start hinting to both Mex and Campbell that the other thinks the other is a wimp or something of that sort. Kinda like that, but it would go like this: 'Hey Mex, Campbell said you weren't as strong as you think. Says he can outlift you on the weights.' The unit had a set of barbells. They were number ten cans filled with cement with a bar extended between them. We used to have contests to see who could curl, military press, or bench press the most. Some strong fuckers in that unit. So Campbell would snort in his superior way and say: 'He's not worth the contest.' Then it just got better and worse.

"After several weeks of this, the fight was on. One afternoon, no missions going, and somehow the two confronted each other. A push, a push back, some words. It was obvious that Campbell didn't want to fight, but he wasn't going to back down either. You didn't become a ranger by being a pussy. You didn't stay a ranger by being a pussy. So they started to punch, wrestle, sand in the face. It was brutal, a collision of titans. Muscle against muscle. Thuds. Smacks. Punches. Sand in the hair. And on and on.

"They got out of breath. They were exhausted after ten minutes. But they kept going. The fight moved from the parade area, and this was in Dong Tam, to the shitters, to the pee tube, to the movie area, to the bunker. It moved on its own depending who backed up, who charged, who punched. And the crowd, about twenty of us, circled and followed. And it didn't end. It went on for three hours, until finally someone called it a draw.

"Everyone still liked Mex after that, but it was Campbell whose esteem soared. He gained the respect of most everyone. We thought he was going to lose, to capsize, to get knocked out. But he was game. Campbell had a new found dignity and he lost a lot of his attitude after that. He was one of the guys. I guess maybe he didn't feel so left out. They were tough fellows. I am glad I didn't have to fight them.

"So this Mex is on my team also for the Bo Bo Canal mission. Wait, another small side story on Mex. On one of the missions months earlier before I got my own team, when Frosty, that is Staff Sergeant Herbert Frost, Old Frosty, was in charge of our hunter-killer missions—those were three teams working together to draw fire and shoot the hell out of the countryside. One team was the hunter, the other two the killers. I was on one of the teams and Mex was on one of the other teams and we were working off the boats. Ours was the 'APL Benewah'. There were five or six APL's or LST's in the Mekong River that went up and down the river from which we operated. We inserted by boat or helicopter. We had previously captured a prisoner, then we had to bring him back to where he had indicated a meeting was going to take place. We set up an ambush, but the P.O.W. lied to us. Frosty apparently ok'd the beheading of the prisoner, and Mex executed the act. I didn't see it, but I did see Mex afterwards with the blood all over him. He was in a blood lust. Seeing him at that time made me realize the wildness of the blood lust. A crazed animal. Frenzied. Totally uncontrollable. So, it is that incident and numerous others that always gave me pause when taking Mex on a mission. What would I do as team leader to control or prevent the outburst of such a blood lust? Could I?"

"He cut his head off? Are you kidding me?" Bob looked incredulous.

"He did it. That's the way it was. Not my order. I had no control. Strange when I think about it. It was a war. Things happen in a war that never happen elsewhere."

"Holy shit!" intoned Bob.

Fred looked at his son. Bob had perked up. There was still a half glass of wine, a water glass at that, but he wasn't drinking too fast. Fred took another sip. The glass dripped on his shirt front; he wiped at it.

"And Frosty was killed, eventually. Had the neatest handlebar mustache you ever saw. Waxed it. And he waxed poetically about being the Legend of the Delta. He thought he was invincible. He wasn't."

"So that was the team: me, Konov, Booth, Moseley as assistant team leader, Koenig, and Mex. Six of us. The perfect ranger team, team 2-1. Experienced, lean, hard, tough, American boys fighting for truth and justice and the American way. I tell you son, you couldn't get a better team. I know some of the other team leaders thought their teams were good, but these guys were the best. And, of course, they had the best team leader. Intelligent, even though I flunked out of college. Tough. Wise decisions,..."

"Ok, pop, cut the crap. Get to the mission. The Bo Bo, or Boo boo, whatever, remember?"

"Heh heh," laughed Fred. He took another sip of wine, condensation dripping.

"Ok, Ok. So I had done the overflight. We prepped for the mission. I got the maps, checked in with the Orderly Room and the First Sergeant, and went over the coordinates. Arranged the coordinates for artillery. We prearranged those so we could call in locations quickly. When you are in a firefight, you don't have time to look for coordinates on a map for artillery. This way we can say the location and the FAC, that is forward air controller, could call it in. We needed a FAC because we were too far out for radio communication with our PRC-25's. The PRC-25 is the radio that I carried as team leader and that the assistant carried. Two radios per team. The range was limited so we needed someone in between us and base. That was the FAC. I have no idea where he was, but they put him somewhere. I don't even remember who was FAC on that mission. Amazing memory, huh? And the PRC-25 weighed seventeen or twenty-five pounds. Don't remember exactly, but it was heavy.

"We had no machine gunner on the mission. We had two M-79 grenade launchers, and one of them was an over and under. M-16 on top, and the grenade launcher underneath. Now that guy carried some ammo. Those grenades are shaped like a bullet, but are forty millimeters in diameter. They are heavy, especially when you carry about fifty of them, and your complement of M-16 magazines. As usual, the M-16 guys took twenty to twenty five magazines. Four or five pouches on their pistol belt. Some guys only put eighteen rounds in a magazine because they believed it would keep the spring in better shape to push up the bullets in the magazine. I kept twenty in each of mine. And to the first one I taped a second one, upside down, so I could easily switch the first magazine if I need it quickly.

"The rest of the guys carried M-16's. I think Booth carried the M-79. Everyone got to select their own headgear. I usually wore a beret. One of our ranger berets with camouflage on the patch. Most guys wore floppy field hats. Some wore helmet liners. Not the steel helmet, just the helmet liner. And on occasion, some would wear the steel pot. It was a motley crew. For awhile I wore a scarf that we had taken off a gook on a mission. Like those scarves that Yasser Arafat wears. A black and white checked scarf. I would put it over my face when I was not on guard, it would keep off the mosquitos. I still have it upstairs."

"I know, I've seen it," said Bob.

"What, you went through my stuff?"

"Dad, I went through it ten years ago. I saw all the pictures too. Of course I did. What did you think I was going to do? Stay out of it. I was curious."

"Oh."

"And I saw the picture of the guy holding up the head of a dead guy by the hair."

"That, son, is the Bo Bo Canal. That, son, is what I am getting at."

"Oh."

Both Fred and Bob took this pause to sip wine. Like coordinated swimming, they both put their glasses down at the same time. Like father, like son.

"So, we ambled over to the helipad. The chopper was already waiting with its blades turning slowly. I get on last, because I always got off first, on the right side. The chopper lifted off, joining four other choppers because they were going to lift the entire platoon out of the area in one pickup. Two Cobra Gunships escorted us; real mean mothers. Three feet wide, they had forty millimeter rockets on both short wings, and a minigun mounted on the lower front nose. The gun alone shot six thousand rounds a minute with six or seven rotating barrels. When it shot at night, with a tracer every fifth round, it looked like a bird peeing from the sky. Boy, those things saved our bacon on a number of occasions. But those are other stories, which, I am sure, at some future time, you will want me to tell you."

"Yeah. But if you keep rambling like you are doing, I don't know if I will ever be able to sit still for so long."

"I guess I am just like my father. God, he used to bore me to tears. But I would just sit and listen. Just like you are going to do now that you got me started, son. Right?"

"Yes father," Bob gave a slight smile, patronizing, yet interested, but not wanting his dad to know it.

"It took half an hour to get to the AO, that is, area of operation. Warm day, the sun getting ready to go down in an hour, breeze blowing though the chopper. You always wanted to make sure you pissed before you got on the chopper. With the cool breeze and the nervous tension, peeing was one of the first things you wanted to do when you landed. Sometimes even before you landed. Especially if it was a hot LZ. That's landing zone, son."

"So, five minutes out, the pilot says we are ready to go in. When we are in the chopper, I put on a headset so I can communicate with the pilot. There is a door gunner on each side of the chopper with an M-60 machine gun mounted on a pod with a bandolier of ammo hooked up so he can go through hundreds of rounds. They have headsets also, so I can listen to the chatter between the gunners and the pilots and the other choppers. So, half a mile away, I took off the headset and got ready to exit.

"I stood on one skid as we came in, the assistant was on the skid on the other side. I can see the troops lined up, three on a side, for the choppers to come in. That way they can scramble on both sides. The choppers don't land, the ground is too wet. They hover, we jump and run past the oncoming troops. We splash in the water that is ankle deep, over the mud and quickly find a small rise that is somewhat dry. We are running in a crouch to keep a low profile, hoping that if the gooks are watching us, that they will only see the confusion of the embarking troops and not the debarking rangers. We lie down, luckily it is dry. The weeds are above our heads. No one can see us."

"The choppers leave in a swirl of mist and noise. It is dead quiet. After listening to the chopper blades and the rushing wind through the open doors of the chopper, the silence is overwhelming. We try to tune in to the quiet. As our senses calm, we become aware of the immediate surroundings. Noises close to us become real noise. Mosquitos discover us. We are a nice local treat after the horrendous blowing about they received from the prop blast of the choppers. We stay still, we listen, we watch. I will wait until dusk hits before we move. We are dry. And, we don't have far to go to the canal. About five hundred meters."

"Sometimes on these stay behind missions, the gooks will come to see whether the troops have dropped grenades or magazines or food. Nothing was moving. The gooks weren't too worried about the troops who were out here, or they didn't care, or they didn't know. I looked over and Koenig was on his side peeing out in front of him. I laughed at that. It's hard enough to pee while kneeling, but to lay on your side. Impressive."

"We were spread out in twos. Never want to isolate any trooper. Always give them support. I am always in the middle, so Moseley would be on one side at the extreme end. As it started to darken, we began to move to our ambush site. I led the way. Mosely was second last. Mex was tail gunner. He was good at that. We walked slowly, looking for booby traps. Didn't expect to find any, but you never know. Had more chance of a booby trap along the canal than out in the watery fields. Keep in mind, this is the Plain of Reeds. It was reedy and plain, flat. As we walked, or stalked, more like it, we kept apart by twenty to thirty feet. That way, if we get shot at, they won't get too many of us in their line of sight. I angled off, then angled back to the canal. Things were clear. The bank was higher than the area we had just traversed. It was about eighteen inches higher than the level of the water in the canal. There was brush and weeds on the bank. We got the clearest spot we could with sufficient weeds so that if there was a moon, we would not be silhouetted."

"It was now about 7:30pm, the area was darkening. It would be pitch black soon. I put Mosely on the far right, then Booth, Konov, me, Koenig and Tex. We had three together, then my three, separated by about six feet. That way, if a couple of sampans came along, we could blow them apart equally. It also allowed us to rotate for guard duty. One man on for two hours, the other two could sleep, if necessary. So two men would always be awake. Nothing happened. Time went on. Mosquitos were fought with ninety-eight percent deet repellant. If you used too much of the stuff for too long, it irritated the hell out of you. It caused abrasions where your skin touched collars, but it worked wonders otherwise. The mosquitos still climbed into our ears and buzzed. You didn't want to put deet too far into your ears. Can't trust those government chemicals too much."

"As time went on, the weather cooled. If you had to pee, you moved to the back of the formation and peed. Far enough away so we didn't have to smell it. Of course far enough away from that location was in the water anyways. But you made sure the person on guard knew you were going to pee. Especially from the other group. Even six feet away, in total darkness it can be a scary surprise if you see your stars blocked out by a moving body. Better to keep people aware of your whereabouts at all times."

"So we are laying there in ambush. Nothing happening. Giving 'sit reps', which are situation reports, to the FAC every hour to let him know we are still alive. Then, about ten minutes before daylight, I get a double squelch on the radio. That means movement. Moseley has spotted something. I look down the canal, less than fifty meters I see a sampan. They are paddling. There are two sampans. They are separated by about fifteen feet. Two men in each sampan, maybe three men in the second sampan. They are rowing with the tide. Even though we are twenty miles from the coast, the tide backs up the Mekong River which causes all the canals to reverse their flow of water. This was the morning tide and the water was rushing towards the Mekong River. In this manner, the gooks floated with the water. Very little rowing other than controlling the direction of the sampan."

"I nudged Koenig, hushed him, he nudged Mex. The first question I asked myself was: Is this an advance party to fifty sampans up the canal, or is this an isolated party that we should just blow away. I looked up the canal. Saw nothing. These guys were now twenty meters and coming smoothly and quietly. Since that time I have canoed in the dark and I know how much noise a canoe makes with the paddles in and out of the water, but at that time I thought they might be able to hear the slightest noise. Guns off safe."

"I am sure Moseley was trying to decide if I had heard his squelchs on the radio and if I was ready to ambush or let them pass. The strict rule for this mission was that I would initiate the contact, if any was to be made. I decided to execute the ambush. It was on. I hunkered lower to the ground."

"The first sampan was level with me. I wanted to let it get a little past me, so the second sampan was in the firing field. When the man in the back of the first sampan was about three feet past me, I put twenty rounds into him and the sampan. All hell broke loose. Everyone fired, there was an explosion from the first sampan. Something in it exploded. Light from the explosion, noise from the guns. The tide kept pulling the sampans. We fired for a full fifteen seconds, then jumped up. Moseley grabbed one of the sampans. The other had sunk or was carried by the swiftly moving water. It was gone.

"One gook was still in the second sampan, dead. We could now see a little more clearly. The sun was emerging and the whole area was becoming lighter. As we looked across the canal, we could see that one of the gooks had climbed the bank and ran into the Plain of Reeds. But we had to make sure that there weren't more gooks coming down the canal. If there were, they would either attack or stop and reverse their sampans. No one wants to float into an ambush."

"Moseley held onto the sampan while we waited for several minutes to see if anything was coming. We saw nothing. Then Mex grabs the dead gook out of the sampan and throws him onto the bank. By now we realized there were no other gooks coming down the waterway. I sent Mosely and Mex across the canal to try to track the running gook. We kept a lookout. We pulled the sampan out of the water onto shore. We started to unload it. It had huge containers made of tin. We pried one open, it held a 122mm rocket. We pried open another size container and it held B-40 rockets. We spread the containers out. These were long sampans, about sixteen to eighteen feet in length. They carried a lot of equipment."

"Moseley and Mex returned after about ten minutes. They lost the trail. There was blood on the trail, but it thinned out and they didn't want to get too far away and get separated, so they returned. As they crossed the canal, they discovered an underwater treasure trove. They put their weapons and web gear on the bank and reentered the water to dip under and get more stuff. Apparently one of the sampans had spilled its booty.

"As they proceeded to gather all the material, I called in the sit rep. Everyone was excited. I kept Koening looking out our back trail and up the canal as we putzed around getting the equipment out of the water. I took out my camera and photographed Mex and Moseley in the water. After wading around, the water came up to their chests, they couldn't find anymore booty, so they came out of the water and put on their gear. You always have to be ready for more action."

"Then, and this is somewhat unusual, Mex grabs the dead gook and starts to dance with him. We all laugh. I make sure Koenig is still on lookout. He is, but he is laughing too. Then Mex says enough of this and tosses the gook. He bounces on the ground once and stops. We laugh. Excitement is high. We are a little unsure of Mex, but we laugh. And maybe it is not we, but me. I remain a little unsure. A cute joke, but really on the edge. And, given the high level of excitement, do you let it go and move on with the mission, or what?"

"Then Koening comes over and pisses in the gooks mouth. I think it was Koening, not entirely sure at this time of my memory. Everyone laughs. I laugh only slightly. Are we getting out of hand? How controllable are these guys? They are extremely excited. Big mission. Getting out of control?

"'Hey pissbreath,' yells someone, directing his comments to the dead gook.

"Mex is in a high state of exhilaration. He looks at the gook and sees a gold tooth and before I see him, he is pounding with his knife butt at the gooks mouth to extract it. Enough. I had had enough of this gratuitous brutality. Even to a dead gook. There was something unseemly about the whole thing and I was increasingly uneasy. It reminded me of the Lord of the Flies. I didn't think of it then, but I have since. You read the book. When all of the kids get into their excited state and they are going to kill Piggy, until the adult comes on the scene and puts sobriety back into the situation. It was the blood lust thing developing. I had to corral it.

"Then Mex pulls the tooth out and says: 'Now I'll get me an ear'. I say, 'Enough'. They look at me. I say "we are not going to be cutting off ears. The tooth is as far as we go. Not on my missions. That's it, we have done enough. You want your picture with the gook, fine, but no abuse of the corpse." Don't know if that was the right term I used, but the meaning was clear. I had put an immediate damper on the excitement. It was at this moment, as I recall later, that command has its dangers. I didn't expect anyone to contradict me and do what they want, but when that blood lust hits, sometimes there is no control. I then, rapidly, redirected the issue."

"'Let's take inventory of this shit and get out of here'. I say. That changed the immediate somberness. Yeah, it was great fun to count the booty. We counted sixty-six B-40 rockets, five 122mm rockets, a couple of AK-47's, and a bunch of miscellaneous shit. The gook had a wallet with a bunch of photos and ID's which we turned in to intel. Then the guys wanted a photo of themselves with the booty, then with the gook. A couple of them held the gook's head up by the hair as they kneeled for their photograph. I had never hunted in civilian life, but I have since then and know where this comes from: deer hunting. When you get a good eight pointer, you want your photo taken with the deer in the field. So these guys wanted their photo taken with their hunting prize. I declined. Again, somewhat unseemly. It seemed to me, and I have thought about it often, that killing another human was dastardly enough. To gloat as if a hunting prize somewhat lessens the cause celebre—that is the reason for being there. And I wonder if I am not just being supercilious, but as I have thought of it over the last thirty years, I think it is an emotion that needs control. And maybe I even let it go too far at that."

"I followed the trial of Lt. Calley. He was the guy, after my time, whose company had a number of people injured by booby traps and who went into the blood lust—that is what I call it—and started to kill all the people in the village; kids, women and old men. I can see how it can happen. If there had been live gooks in our control at that time, what would have happened with the blood lust? I don't want to even surmise. It is unsettling to contemplate."

"So we got extracted, loaded all the booty on the chopper and flew back to Tan An. And what a reception. The First Sergeant and some Intel guys greeted us. It was a grand occasion. They had a steak breakfast for us. It was fun, but it really pissed me off internally. I don't know if it was the reward for a good job, a reward for killing other human beings, and why didn't we get a steak breakfast when we did our usual good job. There was an incongruity about it. Like petting the dog. Good dog, here's a bone. That is just what it was; and, I think that is what pissed me off. Rather than a 'good show old boy', we get a 'good dog, here's a bone.' But that was me. No one else seemed troubled by it. Of course everyone bitched that we didn't always get the steak breakfast, but that was usual."

Bob looked up to see a car coming up the driveway. Fred saw it and picked up his wine glass. Fred was in a high state of excitement. Bob never noticed.

"Dad, it's Barry, I've got to go. We're meeting some kids for basketball. And hey, thanks for the story. It's great to hear one of them finally. Gotta go." Bob bolted from the room.

Fred commiserated. Gee whiz, I must be as boring as my own father. God, what a time. What do those guys think of what we did then? And here I am telling war stories, just like my own father.

Epilogue

If you are a Ranger of Co. E, then this book has assuredly brought home to you some little details you completely forgot about Dong Tam, Tan An, or the area in general. In addition, I am sure it has stirred your blood about your time in Vietnam, about the friendships you forged, and the friends you lost.

I have met many veterans since Vietnam. Some talk of their experiences, some do not. Some brag about their experiences, and some apologize. Not everyone was a combat vet. We read of homeless veterans on public assistance and we generalize about veterans. But, the veterans are the core of this country; they did what they were requested to do and required to do.

The ability to talk about the war reflects the attitude and ability of the veteran to cope with what the war did to him; and, maybe, what he did in the war. There were things we did, especially in our type of work, that we choose to forget, or, maybe even to repress. But we talked about it; the war, our role in it, what was important to us, what the impact was on us, and what it did to us. As a result, an impression of our involvement formed. After all, who really cares if Newman got into a fight with a Yankee hating hillbilly; he doesn't even remember the guy's name? Well, I can tell you, Newman cares. He can't remember the guy's name, but he surely remembers the event. That event, a war within a war, a war of a hundred and ten years ago still engendering such vitriolic hate, that had a significance to Newman and no one else. It had an impact on him that caused him to look at people differently. To see where they came from. What mores, culture, and pressures were inflicted on those people merely by virtue of birth in a certain location? To see that hate and prejudice can be prevalent anywhere, if the person allows it. Each event that occurs to a person or as a result of that person's action, is what gives us our attitude and approach to the war thirty-two years later.

It was our war, our remembrances, our legacy. I congratulate each of you for your participation. In the event we have offended anyone, it was certainly not intentional. A certain hyperbole needed to be utilized to make certain points, but that was literary license so needed to make a book interesting. We hope you have enjoyed your reading, we enjoyed the presentation.

The authors

About the Authors

JACK BICK

Jack Bick is the publisher of *Inside Collin County Business*, a monthly business newspaper started in 1994 to report of business in one of the fastest growing markets in the country, Collin County, Texas.

Jack is a graduate of the University of Missouri School of Journalism and served as a reporter for the U.S. Army in Vietnam where he was decorated for valor as well as journalistic endeavors.

His career has included work in community newspapers and local business journals involving assignments in reporting, circulation, advertizing and administration. He is known for successful start-ups and turn-arounds especially in the business journal area.

He has been married for thirty-one years to Angie. They have three grown children, Cindy, John, and Sam, and one grandchild, Justin. They live in McKinney, Tx. Both Jack and his wife are involved in may community and church related activities.

BOB WALLACE

Bob Wallace needed money after being discharged from the U.S. Army in May, 1970. He returned to graduate school on the GI Bill for three months, briefly worked for a congressman, then, in part because he was a Vietnam Veteran, obtained employment with the Central Intelligence Agency. In 2001, he received a 30-year service pin.

Mr. Wallace could not have had the Vietnam experience except in the Spring of 1968, the Lincoln County draft board declared that "six years in college is enough for anyone from Barnard, Kansas."

He may not have obtained a graduate degree from the University of Kansas save for a thesis committee, in June 1968, that felt sympathy for anyone who lost educational deferment for reasons other than unsatisfactory grades.

He could not have survived Vietnam during 1969 except for the brotherhood of the 75th Infantry LRRP's and the grace of God.

Without an involuntary year long separation from a pretty social worker, Mary Margaret Shaw, he likely would have failed to realize how wonderful life could be with her or enjoy the happiness of their three children.

Mr. Wallace would never have written any of these stories had not Paul Newman come up with the idea and pushed him to get them done.

PAUL A. NEWMAN

Having dropped out of Bowling Green State University for lack of money and grades, Paul worked in a factory as a grinder. Seeing no future there, he joined the army three months before his projected draft date.

After qualifying for Airborne, he was assigned to Ft. Bragg in January, 1968. With no leave, the 3rd Brigade was airlifted to Vietnam for Tet, 1968. His second tour was voluntary, with the Co. E, 75th Inf., 9th Inf. Div.. After he was wounded, he received an early out.

Paul then decided he may be mature enough to go to college. He attended Case Western Reserve University, received a Bachelor's Degree, then a Master's Degree. Then he went to Cleveland State University Law School. His wife wondered if he would ever stop going to school. He did stop, finally.

He practices law in Chardon, Ohio with a small firm in a small town: Newman & Brice.

Paul has written a novel, *Joe B,* published by Iuniverse.com. It is a modern day parallel of the life of Job.

He is also an amateur photographer having won numerous local competitions. His photo of a waterfall in Vietnam won Best of Show at the Great Geauga County Fair in 1999.

He is extensively involved in his community. He has been a Rotarian for the past twenty years and a member of various Boards. He also serves on his local Veterans Service Commission. He is a member of DAV, American Legion, VVA, and VFW

Paul has been married to Merrilou for thirty-two years; they have two daughters.

0-595-25305-9